Neil Quinn

THE

Fat Ladz!

TRAIN TRACKS, TRAINING AND TURF WARS

Contents

Chapter One

Paul stood at the bottom of the cold steel steps, pulling hard on his fourth cigarette of a wet March morning. It was five forty-five. His twelve-hour shift was beginning at six. Determined not to use the lift, he threw the stub onto the concrete and stamped on it.

He stared blankly forward, the rain soaking his thick dark hair, and gasped as he took the initial steps to lumber up to the first landing. The breath whistled from his lungs as he gripped the handrail to scale the second flight. This was his exercise for the day, and he rested at the top of the third set of steps until sure he could open the door without panting or fainting and enter, calm and relaxed. Deep breath. Calm and relaxed. Scan the card. Open the door. Calm and relaxed. Enter.

'Fuck, look at the state of you. 'Ave you just run a marathon, or what?' was Carl's welcome on the other side.

Paul opened his mouth to reply but couldn't catch his breath, and Carl was on his way home anyway so wasn't hanging around for an answer.

Hating this daily nightmare, Paul stood for a few seconds to let his heart slow. He dropped his bag in the breakout room and, still winded from his efforts, headed gingerly to the operating floor to relieve one of the nightshift. Dudley had already arrived on Centre when Paul signed in on the West, but poor Bobby Brown on the East end was waiting for Tiler.

By the time Tiler arrived, Paul had already drunk his tea and was going through his paperwork for the day. The rain was still dripping from Tiler's bulldog head onto his scruffy donkey jacket as he relieved an annoyed Bobby Brown. Tiler was always the last to arrive.

'One minute to six! How the *fuck* d'you manage that every day, Tiler? You really are a fat, lazy twat,' Bobby moaned as he glared at the clock, looking exhausted. Tiler laughed and bowed, while Paul and Dudley added their opinion in no uncertain terms.

When the noise had died away, Bobby Brown talked Tiler through the night shift and made a hasty exit, ten minutes late. 'Prick!' he uttered as he disappeared out the door.

Tiler threw his wet coat under his desk and noisily began to adjust his chair. 'These fuckin' chairs are crap,' he declared loudly, slamming it down on its wheels to make it tilt. After a short altercation with the unfortunate chair, he dropped himself into it. 'And they get smaller every fuckin' day!'

He banged down the headrest with a fist, threw his feet up onto the desk and looked across at Paul. 'What?' he said innocently.

Paul shook his head slowly and averted his gaze.

The Rail Operating Centre, a modern signal box, could be a quiet place, and such was the case this morning. Time passed as the three signallers monitored their workstations, each position housing assorted electronic equipment and numerous telephones below screens that showed the tracks, the signalling and the location of trains covering hundreds of miles. The responsibility for all these trains and the lives of thousands of passengers and staff lay in the hands of those working here.

'So, this is how we move a set of points,' Paul was saying to the new management and technical training intern, a slim young guy with natural blonde corkscrew hair and bright blue eyes, 'but to be honest, we don't normally touch them. We leave it to the ARS.'

'The arse?'

'Yeah, the ARS. A-R-S, actually – Automatic Route Setting.'

The trainee giggled. 'So, you use the ARS in the Central Rail

Operating Centre – the CROC? The ARS in the CROC!'

'I know – you couldn't make it up. Of all the things they could've called it! We only step in when there's a problem that the system can't deal with or something unusual.'

'Like what?' asked the trainee.

'A broken-down train or something on the line, perhaps. Or engineering work. It can go from zero to a hundred miles an hour at any moment, but until then, I suppose you could say we're like system monitors.'

'D'you get breaks?'

'Of course. One of the relief guys comes in to cover. We generally go and sit in the breakout room – read the paper or something. We should go for a walk, stretch our legs, but nobody does.'

'You don't do your ten thousand steps a day doing this job, then?'

Paul laughed. 'It's sedentary, for sure.' He pointed towards the breakout room. 'They've put a vending machine in there now, which doesn't do anyone any favours, er, sorry, what was your name?'

'I don't think I'll be staying here long, then. I need something more active. That's what my mum says, anyway.' The intern looked around thoughtfully.

'We were young once too, y'know,' said Paul. 'Most of us came from working the old-fashioned lever-frame signal boxes. They kept us active, plus we worked on the track sometimes, so it was always physical. You might have enjoyed that work. This is a whole different ball game.'

'Maybe. But now the computer does all the work, and you just sit and wait for something to go wrong?'

Paul shrugged. 'Exactly that,' he replied as they watched Tiler finally extricating himself from his chair. Tiler stood, stretched and rubbed his eyes, then closed the blinds against the early-morning sun bursting through the window. He wandered over to Dudley's desk and stole a chocolate Hobnob from his colleague's ever-present packet.

Dudley was busy on the phone berating a contractor who was

giving him a list of track works that would ensure he went home with a headache. He was the oldest and most experienced operator in the ROC and was open about approaching retirement with mixed feelings. Dour and dishevelled, and known never to use ten words when one would do, he loved his job and was reliable, conscientious and enthusiastic.

Behind the vast array of screens and monitors, the big orange *Breakout Area* sign glowed.

'I'll never know why they felt the need to change that, Paul,' said Tiler while he munched on another biscuit off Dudley's desk.

Paul knew what was coming. Tiler had been through this a thousand times.

'I mean – what's the matter with *Rest Room* like it's always been called? They tart it up, and now it's a fuckin' *Breakout Area*. I don't go there to break out; I go to rest. It's bollocks!' Paul was long past answering, but Tiler carried on anyway. 'I mean, why do they change stuff all the time? *Signaller* – what's that all about? I'm a signalman – always have been, always will be. Such shit.'

As no one was biting, Tiler moved on. 'Anyone cooking this morning?' he asked optimistically.

'If you get the food on your break, I'll cook for everyone,' said Daniel, who had arrived to do his assessments on the computer.

Daniel, neatly turned out in clean, sharply pressed company chinos and navy T-shirt, was serious about food. He was serious about pretty much everything, but particularly food. He was known as the 'ROC chef' and could turn his hand to anything in the kitchen. After meals, it was often suggested that Daniel should be on *MasterChef* and that his talents were wasted working on the railway. He really was that good. But he was quiet and introverted and not that confident in his abilities.

'Awesome! I was thinking eggs, bacon, sausage, beans, mushies and toast?' Tiler said, rubbing his hands.

'Hash browns?'

'Now you're talking my language!' Dudley slobbered and

wiped his mouth, suddenly energised.

By the time Tiler had returned, lugging the shopping bags that bulged with their breakfast, Bethan, the newest addition to the ROC, had arrived to cover their break. As Daniel began his magic, the aroma from the kitchen drifted onto the operating floor.

'Wow,' the management and technical training intern said. 'Do you do this every day?'

'Pretty much,' replied Paul. 'Depends whether we've got a chef on, but definitely when Daniel is around. Pure quality; just give it a sniff!'

'I love the smell, but I'm afraid it's too much food for me,' said Bethan.

Within twenty minutes, piled-high plates started to arrive at their desks, and they were as promised. The eggs were perfect and clean, the bacon not too soft but not crisp, the sausages beautifully brown with a little fat dripping off the ends, all accompanied by beans, mushrooms and enough buttered toast to feed a small army. There was even a massive mug of hot tea each to wash it all down. Nobody uttered a word for the next twenty minutes.

And then it was over, leaving everyone bouncing and ready for the challenges of the day.

'Well?' said Paul.

'That was pretty amazing,' the trainee replied enthusiastically, sipping on his passionflower tea. 'It's not surprising you're all so ...' His words faded into the carpet as the room fell silent. A telephone rang, relieving the tension, and everyone returned to work.

Daniel returned to the operating floor. 'What's the verdict?'

'Good,' 'Yeah, fine,' and 'OK, thanks, Daniel,' was the unusually muted response.

'Wish I hadn't bothered,' Daniel muttered.

*

'So, you think we're a load of fat bastards, do you?' Tiler said to the trainee. It was lunchtime, and Tiler had clearly been stewing on this since breakfast.

'Of course, not … you're just … in … in a job that's … well … sedentary.' The pauses were a little too long, but the intern had struck a nerve. They often discussed that their health was deteriorating, their weight was rising, and their well-being was beginning to suffer.

Tiler carried on as if the trainee hadn't spoken. 'Most of us have been fit all our lives – rugby, football, cricket – you name a sport, and someone up here will have played it: Carl, a judo black belt; Kev, first-choice scrum half – he could've gone all the way except for injury; I used to be a goalkeeper; Andy, a champion boxer in the Army; and most of us played football, some to a high level. So, for you to come in here, accusing us of being fat and out of condition …'

The trainee was sitting way back in his seat.

'Leave him alone. You know he's right,' Paul said.

Daniel folded his arms. 'Sorry for making such great food!'

'You *do* know he's right, Tiler,' Paul continued, not happy that Tiler was taking his problems out on the intern. 'It was only last week we were saying we were fed up with not being able to climb the steps, having to rest on benches while out walking and struggling for breath at the slightest exertion. That's exactly what we spoke about. Then you agreed and said how fit and fearless you used to be playing Sunday League. Oh, ye of short memory!'

Tiler didn't reply. He took a deep breath and returned to his workstation. 'These chairs are fuckin' crap!' he barked, slamming the miserable chair into the floor.

*

Paul went through the conversation again as he wandered round the shops on his afternoon break. He was not as out of condition or overweight as Tiler, but he knew he was on the slippery slope.

The latest computer upgrade meant they were doing even less on their workstations and becoming lazy owing to the static nature of the job. Add to that the food they were putting away, lack of exercise, staring at computer screens and instant stress when the sticky stuff hit the fan – it all made for a dangerously unhealthy and toxic blend.

Paul thought about some of the others.

Trev, for instance. Great guy: he'd give you his last penny. Not as young as he used to be but always smart and quick to help anyone. Walked with a limp that looked horribly painful. Rumour had it he once tried out for Bristol Rovers, but nobody knew the full story.

Kev, or Clown Kev to his mates. Whenever there were shenanigans or pranks, Kev always seemed to be involved. It had got to the point he was blamed for anything, whether he was involved or not.

When at signing-off time, Dudley couldn't find his old bike to ride home, and it was eventually found on the roof of an adjacent building, Clown Kev had been on shift and always denied being involved.

When sugar was replaced with salt in the sugar bowl, causing two of them to throw up, Clown Kev had been on shift and always denied being involved.

When pornographic pages from a magazine were ripped out and stuck into a book of rules and regs, Clown Kev had been on shift and always denied being involved.

With his sandy, poker-straight hair that touched his shoulders, Kev was always smiling and always on the go. There was never a dull moment when he was around. He had come into the job after spending several years as a warehouse manager. Unfortunately, he was found solely responsible for said warehouse burning down one night. They didn't prosecute as he had been a good employee. After eighteen months, they gave him his job back, but within a year the warehouse had burnt down again. He narrowly missed being put away for several years, thanks to a technicality.

Paul himself was a natural leader and had been identified by management for higher things. He had the feel for authority. He'd been on all the courses but that was just for the overtime; he wasn't interested in moving up. Promotion wasn't on his agenda. He was happy at home with his wife, Paula, and now that their two busy boys had started in the Comp, life was getting easier. But, like most of them, he was now middle-aged, and it was starting to show. When he looked in the mirror, he could see his once coal-black hair beginning to speckle and his cheeks starting to sag. He often thought about how to turn it around.

*

'OK, so it's like this – I'm not getting any younger and neither are you lot. Most of us are a stone too heavy, and it's not pretty. Some of us have got kids, and if this carries on, we're not going to see them grow up. I'm fed up with seeing you all wandering round with your fat arses hanging out and the grease running down your double chins from breakfast.

'We've got to try and turn this around – make ourselves healthier before it's too late. We're in a pressurised environment all day or night, and we need something to calm us down, otherwise we'll end up with high blood pressure and stuff. We can have some fun doing it, though. We just have to find something interesting enough to keep us involved. Simple as. What d'you reckon?'

'Stick it up your arse!'

That's roughly how Paul figured that conversation would go as he rushed back to work. He scurried through the rain, angry that he was panting. He knew it was going to be a hard sell, as everyone had pretty much settled down. That was part of the problem. Contentment had led to expanded waistlines. The easy life.

He remembered how, just a few years earlier, he would skip up the steps to the ROC and bound through the door with hardly a care. Nowadays, the climb left him gasping. Once again, he started up the three short flights. At the top this time, he stopped, lit a cigarette and put it to his mouth.

'This has got to go,' he said, looking at the cigarette like an old friend.

He took a huge drag, pulled the smoke deep into his lungs, held it there for what little time he could, and then blew it out hard.

He threw the rest of the cigarette onto the step and stamped on it, twisting his foot to grind it through the grating. Turning to scan in, he caught his reflection in the window. He paused, then went in, slamming the door behind him.

*

'For Christ's sake, Paul,' screamed Tiler from the breakout room. 'You nearly took that fuckin' door off its hinges!'

'Just really cheesed off,' said Paul, joining Tiler and heading to his locker.

'You didn't get it again last night, then?' Tiler laughed, simulating sex with his fingers.

Tiler didn't worry about anyone and didn't want anyone to be worried about. He was married once, but his wife left him. The final straw had come when she'd organised a fitter to finish off her dream kitchen with designer wall tiles. But Tiler found out and cancelled him to 'save a few bob', attempting it himself. That finished with more tiles smashed on the floor than were on the wall. Add on the extra cost of patching up the mess, and it was, 'more than I can take, you miserable bastard!' Since then, he'd been known as 'Tiler'. In fact, many didn't even know his real name.

Paul sighed. 'I'm just fed up with the monotony – home to work, work to home, feed the kids, taxi the kids, get the kids to bed, fall asleep in front of the telly, go to work, *ad nauseum*. Really need something to give me a reason, something to look forward to, something to wake me up,' he said.

'You've got us and this place, haven't you? What more could

you possibly need in life?'

'Yeah, thanks for that,' Paul said with a grimace.

'Anyways, you'd better get out the front. Trev's got a load of trouble waiting for you.'

'You're jokin' me.'

'No, the bastards have stolen our power cables down at the junction again – lots of fuckin' trains on lots of fuckin' stop for you.'

Paul filled his water bottle. 'Bugger, that's the last thing I need today, or any day.' He was still muttering to himself as the door eased quietly shut behind him.

*

Paul didn't have time to think much more. Before he knew it, time had passed and things on the track were getting back to normal.

'Ready for a break, Paul?'

Paul jumped at Andy's voice right behind him. Andy – stocky, squat, ex-forces – had a thing about walking quickly and quietly. Everyone thought it was from his days in the Army; they were pretty certain he'd been SAS. He'd kept his tight crew cut and had strong features and piercing blue eyes that looked right into your soul. He was as straight as they come and didn't waste time with niceties.

'Your turn for a brew, mate.'

'Right, thanks, Andy. Listen, I need to speak to you after. There are a couple of things I've been thinking about; need a few ideas. OK?'

'No probs; happy to help.'

'Great, thanks.'

He took Andy through what was happening on the tracks and left him to it.

*

In the breakout room, Paul began his speech, but he wished he had a bigger audience. Just Tiler and Bethan stared back at him blankly. He didn't even get the 'stick it up your arse' that he was expecting, but, on the upside, they had listened and accepted much of what he said.

Bethan, her fair hair cut into a boyish style over her freckled face, was new to the work and keen – not yet dragged down by deskbound stresses and strains. Much younger than the rest, she was the future – very switched on, sharp, active and no wilting violet. As a prison officer, she had thought nothing of taking on inmates bigger than herself and had played for the Prison Service rugby team. She'd gained a lot of respect from her new colleagues in a short time.

'What about we start a running club?' she suggested. 'Those who can't run can start with walking – see how they get on – Couch to 5K-type thing. My mother's doing it and doing OK – or would be if she laid off the Jaffa Cakes.'

'Wouldn't work,' Paul said. 'It's too boring, and on cold, rainy days, we'd soon drop out and go back to square one. It's got to be something that gives us an interest – more than just exercise.'

'I agree,' chipped in Tiler. 'All the runners I know are so self-obsessed; they can only talk about running and their injuries.' Mimicking one in a singing whine, he droned, '"I pulled my hamstring taking a second off my 10K time," and all I want to say is, "I don't give a fuck. Get a life, you self-centred, sanctimonious twat!" Running is running is running – it's shit.'

'Whoa. Calm down, Tiler,' Paul said. 'I think we get the message. Not running, then.'

Andy walked in and glided to the sink without a sound.

'What's happening here?' he asked, filling the kettle. 'You said you wanted me, Paul. What did you want to talk about?'

'I was just saying this place is dragging everyone down. So many of us are becoming fat; even you've put on a bit of timber since you've been here. And most of us are unhealthy – bored, even – you know, just going through the motions.'

'… like a sewage inspector …' Tiler interjected.

Paul shut him up with a glance. 'Well, rugby and boxing were my things but obviously out of the question.'

Having just taken a handful of biscuits out of the tin, Andy looked at them thoughtfully then put half of them back. 'Have you thought about football? You could have some fun while getting fit and maybe lose a bit of weight.'

'I don't think we could get eleven players, and no one could last ninety minutes!' replied Paul.

'What about six-a-side?' said Bethan. 'I used to play in a team when I was in prison' – that's how she referred to her time there – 'and we used to have a great laugh.'

'That would be a possibility – what with everyone working shifts – and it'd be a shorter game,' Paul said. 'Actually, d'you know what? That's a brilliant idea!'

'I haven't kicked a ball since God was a boy,' Tiler groaned.

'It's like riding a bike,' said Andy. 'Tighten up a few muscles and ligaments, and you'll be straight back into it!'

'Right,' said Paul. 'I'll have a look around for a club and see what we've got to do.'

'No need,' said Bethan. 'There's a league down at the Rec. They're probably well into the season, but I saw a sign up outside the Football Centre when I drove past the other day. That's what made me think of it.'

'Brilliant. What d'you think? Everyone in?'

They all nodded.

'Awesome,' said Paul, rubbing his hands. 'I'll call down there asap and find out what the score is, then we can start recruiting.'

'*We*?' Tiler came to life. 'I didn't say I'd be organising this!'

'You're such a lazy sod, Tiler. Come on, make an effort at something that doesn't end in you screwing things up!' Paul paused and took a breath. 'What do you guys say?'

'Let's do it,' Andy said. Tiler nodded along, still not completely sold.

*

'Where the fuck have you been? You should have been back on shift ten minutes ago! D'you know what, Paul? You people treat this place like you fuckin' own it. You've knocked the relief schedule right off, and Dudley's going to be fifteen minutes late coming back, which means Andy can claim fifteen minutes' overtime. D'you know what, if he does, it'll come out of your wages, you can be sure of that!'

Everybody's friend, Gerry Spratt, stared at the latecomers, red-faced. He was the recently promoted ROC manager – poacher turned gamekeeper, if ever there was one.

Paul didn't feel his reply would be appropriate, so he stayed quiet and carried on with his work, while Gerry took the chance to quarrel with anyone who expressed an opinion. He was relatively old to be promoted, but the manager's job was so demanding, nobody else had applied for it. With no empathy or people skills, no one was a more inappropriate manager than Gerry Spratt. It was no secret he'd only gone for the position to enhance his pension. A perfect storm.

'Gerry Spratt – the fish out of water,' they'd laugh.

He became even more insufferable when he started to wear a suit and tie to work. He was extremely partial to a cooked breakfast, and unfortunately, grease from a Benny's bacon roll that morning had oozed onto his company tie, ruining the look. He didn't notice – or care, for that matter. The tie was only there to cover his belly button, which often made an appearance above a strained waistband.

Gerry worked his way round each section in turn, doing his manager's checks. Each operator he upset, he seemed to consider a bonus, allowing him to go back to his office a happy man.

Tiler, Bethan, Dudley and Paul endured his barbs until the management and technical training intern whispered to Paul, 'My God, do people like this still exist? It's like something out of a seventies sitcom!'

'What are you whispering about?' Gerry shouted from the other side of the room, narrowing his already narrow piggy eyes. 'D'you know what? When I get settled into this job, you lot are going to see a different side of me, and you won't like it. You'll get away with nothing. I've got my eye on all of you; you can be sure of that!" He threw them an 'I'm watching you' gesture.

The door slammed shut behind him.

'The ROC cock,' said Tiler, and suddenly everyone was laughing.

Chapter Two

O nce home, Paul began to make a list of those in the ROC who were physically able and likely to be interested in his idea. He figured he could make it work with a shortlist of eight or nine, allowing for shifts and unavailability.

So far, he knew Andy, Bethan and himself were on board. Tiler, with one more push, would be too.

Bobby Brown – he would be up for it, for sure. Not so fat and loved his football. Put him down as a definite.

Trev – everyone had heard he'd been a good footballer, but his foot problems meant he could barely walk now, never mind play a match. So that would be a 'no' for him.

Then there was Gav – sport crazy, always on about football, but could he play? It was worth asking.

Carl was a gym freak, more interested in working out than football. But his experience from his days doing security and being a bouncer in the pubs and clubs might help to get it all going.

Lastly, Kev – Clown Kev – couldn't open his mouth without putting his foot in it. He was always involved when something was bubbling.

Paul picked up his phone. He'd start ringing around to see if he could raise some interest and get the numbers he needed to organise a slot in the league at the Rec.

*

'You can stick that right up your arse!'

Paul smiled. It was his first 'you can stick that right up your arse!' of the evening.

'If you think I'm working all day, then running up and down a bloody football pitch making a twat of myself ...!'

'Your name is 'Clown Kev', so don't worry about that – people think you're a twat already.' Paul said this more as a statement of fact than a dig, and Kev seemed to accept it as such. 'I'll put you down as a "maybe", then.'

'Yeah, maybe – and maybe not!' Then he was gone, leaving Paul staring at his phone.

'Damn,' he hissed under his breath.

But, overall, he was pleased, as none of those he'd contacted was an out-and-out 'no'. So far, he had eight names, including himself, and he planned to get down to the Rec the following day to register the team for the league which had begun some months previously. It was starting to look like a goer.

They could get some training sessions in, and however it went, it would be good to spend time with the guys outside the ROC. They weren't a bad lot, but there were always some colleagues you liked more than others. There wasn't much chance of that idiot of a manager creating any bonding sessions for them, that was for sure. With luck, they might even make the National Newsletter. What could possibly go wrong?

*

Trev was musing on how quickly a week passed for shift workers – no sooner had one roster been published than another Thursday dawned, and the next roster arrived. Time appeared accelerated, which led to many overstaying their welcome: 'How long have you been doing this job?' 'Six months ... two years ... ten years ...

thirty years!' It happened so quickly; it was hard to know where it all went.

That was how Trev felt. His advice to new arrivals was always the same: 'Get some experience, then move on. Get out while you're young, otherwise the place will overpower you.'

It could have been so different. He had been ecstatic when he went for his trial at Bristol Rovers; each player had stars in their eyes, but he knew he was better than all of them. He found football so easy. He was flying, regal, with so much more time on the ball than the others. The coaches made notes every time he touched the ball.

And then, that life-changing tackle – he could still feel the studs burning down his calf, tearing into the muscle, then penetrating deep behind his Achilles tendon, severing it above the heel, followed by the sound of a whip cracking as his ankle splintered into jagged pieces piercing his skin. So much blood, so much pain, all the horrified faces and then the release when he eventually passed out. Not only did it finish his trial, it finished any hopes he had of ever playing football again. After all the operations, they told him in no uncertain terms that just being able to walk would be the target now.

On the scrapheap at nineteen with a limp, he took the first job to come along. Signalling shunting operations in the marshalling yards – it was a hard landing. But it was a job – he'd just use it as a stopgap. Now, thirty years later, he was still there.

'Fuck 'em!' Trev was often heard to say for no apparent reason. 'Fuck 'em all!'

He was pondering this and about to say, 'Fuck 'em!' when Paul burst into the breakout room.

'I've done it – I've gone ahead and done it!'

Tiler, sitting opposite Trev, jerked upright. 'What? What have you done?'

'I've signed us up.' Blank faces all round. 'The football! I've booked our place in the league. We're starting a bit late in the season, but it's going to be brilliant down there. Astroturf, floodlights, café, bar, everything! We start next week. Need to sort out a team …'

'Whoa, whoa, whoa. I thought we were going to have a few weeks to train and get fit!' said Tiler.

'You'll need a bit of fitness,' agreed Trev.

'Well, there's no time like the present, so I'll see who's available for the first match. Pity we're not going to get you down there, Trev. It's against the No-Hopers, so I reckon we're in with a shout.'

'Yeah, if only I could,' Trev replied, staring sadly at his ever-painful ankle.

'Sounds like a shitstorm to me,' muttered Tiler, always the optimist.

'Fuck 'em,' said Trev quietly. 'Fuck 'em all.'

*

It was Saturday. Paul had been working all week to get a team together for the match on Monday evening. After speaking to Tiler and Trev, Paul had seen Gav as he was leaving work. He was right up for it. He loved football – hadn't played in a team, but how hard could it be? He was a thirty-something petrol-head who loved buying and selling; it was his dream to get on *The Apprentice* so he could make his first million.

'But if Tiler gives me any shit, I'm walking off – defo!'

You could say that Gav and Tiler didn't get on, but that would hide the fact that no one got on with Tiler.

'Don't worry; no one will be giving anyone any shit. It's just going to be a lot of fun.'

Next had been a call to Bethan. She was a bit concerned about her fitness level but prepared to give it a go. Bethan loved a challenge, and if it involved taking it to the men, she was doubly determined.

Bobby Brown was the next call. He needed no persuading,

as he was always looking for a legitimate excuse to get out of the house. His (well-known and much-discussed) weakness was women. He loved women and, to be truthful and fair, women loved him. Whether it was the bright-blue eyes, the short, professionally groomed beard or the dark complexion, nobody knew. He was an outrageous flirt if a female had the misfortune to be in his presence, and one day it would surely be his downfall.

Being married wasn't a barrier to Bobby; he'd had more girlfriends than Charlie Sheen. In fact, his colleagues had occasionally answered the buzzer to women asking for Bobby and found themselves telling lies to save his neck. Or, even worse, his wife calling in because Bobby had said he was in work when he was elsewhere. He had been told on several occasions that next time, he would be shopped, but realistically that was never going to happen. He was such a nice guy and had the knack of keeping everyone onside. Quite the Lothario, Bobby Brown.

Paul had seen Andy on his next shift. They spoke for most of the day about the match – tactics, cheap ways to score goals, keeping the effort to a minimum and doing just enough to win until they were fitter. Very positive.

Although he only needed six players, at some stage they'd need a break, so he would use the extra player to work that in. Kev had been next on his tick list. Always a joy to talk to Kev. He was not as negative as the last time Paul had spoken to him and appeared flattered Paul had thought of him. He even said he was looking forward to it.

That gave Paul the seven he needed to play on Monday. He'd asked them all to bring a blue shirt, and he dug out an old large green T-shirt for the keeper to wear. He was quite excited that he had lifted everyone's spirits.

'Roll on Monday!' he said, settling back in his chair.

*

Monday came round fast, and Paul was back in work. Word had spread about the match; everyone was talking about it. Even those with no interest in football were asking questions.

Samantha, who worked in all three ROCs – East, West and Central – as required, had just come back off maternity leave. 'So, you're playing six-a-side, and you've got seven to have a sub – that's not much rest if you're knackered,' she said.

'I agree,' said Paul, 'but if we can get in a few early goals, we can sit back on them. One sub should be enough.'

'Put me and Andy up front. We'll bang in a few while you guys cover the back,' suggested Bethan.

'Sounds great,' Paul said. 'We'll start with Tiler in goal and see where we go from there. It's ten minutes each way with two minutes for half-time, so plenty of time to switch around.'

'I've seen some of the guys,' Bethan added, 'and they're quite excited but a bit nervous as they haven't done anything like this. That'll pass as soon as we kick off, for sure.'

'Great,' said Paul. 'That's what we're trying to do, after all – push our boundaries and do something different. Try and create a bit of camaraderie, even with those who don't play. Bonding, if you like.'

'Hey, don't get involved with all that stuff – I've seen pictures!' shouted Sam, and everyone laughed.

'*Bonding*, not bondage!' Paul was laughing too. 'I'll run through the rules on the night so every—'

He was interrupted by the slamming of the door. Sam looked down and shook her head. 'Oh, no,' she uttered under her breath. 'This is the only thing I hate about working here.'

Gerry Spratt appeared from behind the screens.

'No, you sort it out!' he was shouting into his phone. 'I know you're only going sick to make things difficult for me, so you ring round for cover. I'm a manager, not a supervisor in a fucking crèche!' He jabbed at the red circle on his screen.

'Prick! Must think I came up on the down train. Well, I'll tell you what – I've been around long enough to know all the tricks, so don't any of you lot try that one … not on me! I'm fed up with people taking the piss at every opportunity. I *cannot* understand why you people can't just come to work, do your job and bugger off home. Is that too much to ask? Instead, you want to make my life as difficult as possible. Daniel on the phone, "Oh, my daughter's ill,"' Gerry said in his mocking voice. "'I need some time off." Ha! I've got problems, more than any of you lot, but I'm always in work. Why can't everyone be like me?'

'God forbid,' Sam whispered behind Paul.

Everyone was shaking their heads. It was common knowledge that Daniel's daughter, Emily, was poorly, and it drained him a bit more every day. To avoid upsetting Gerry, he often came into work when he should have been at home.

Gerry wasn't finished. 'Compassionate leave, he said! No, go sick, and then they can see your crappy attendance when you go for promotion. That'll teach you all to try and screw *me* over!'

He started his weekly checks at Samantha's desk and was mercifully quiet for a while. Then he started on a different tack. 'What's this football thing you've got going on?' he asked no one in particular.

Paul answered, even though he didn't want to get into the conversation. 'I've organised a six-a-side team to play in the League down at the Rec. Got a good team, I think – should be fun.'

Gerry silently carried on with his workstation checks until he finished at Paul's desk. 'Fun? *Fun?* You lot are gonna be shit; most of you can't even get up the steps, never mind play a football match. Just a bunch of middle-aged fat lads trying to relive their youth. I should come and watch. It's gonna be hilarious!'

Paul didn't respond. No one ever argued with Gerry. This wasn't because they were afraid to, but more that arguing or disputing his proclamations and assertions would somehow give them credence. Arguing would give the appearance his words were important in some way, so it was rare that anyone would bite, no matter how provocative, annoying and infuriating Gerry became.

'What time are you playing?'

Paul hesitated. Gerry was the last person he, or any of them for that matter, wanted there. 'Seven o'clock,' he answered grudgingly.

'If I can get away, I'll be there. Wouldn't miss this for the world. You lot making complete pricks of yourselves. Ha!' The door slammed as he left.

Only the intern had outwardly been paying any attention to Gerry's rant. 'Are all managers like that here? I'm starting to think of looking somewhere else for a career. And why is he so scathing about the football?'

'Sod him. Just go and enjoy it,' said Samantha wisely. 'Sorry, I didn't catch your name, but enjoyment and satisfaction are what it's all about at the end of the day. If you can meet with success and failure and treat them both the same, then you're much better than I am – or something like that.'

'That's pretty sage,' said Paul.

'Great life advice, too!' agreed Bethan.

'I'd like to take the credit, but it's a quote,' said Sam. 'Shakespeare, I think.'

It took a while for everyone to come round after Gerry's visit, which would no doubt have pleased him immensely. Before long they had all left, and the new shift had begun.

Chapter Three

Paul's stomach was doing somersaults as he walked from a wet winter's night into the Rec's expansive foyer, then through automatic sliding glass doors into the Football Centre. None of the others were there yet.

The atmosphere buzzed in the cool, fresh air. He looked round the warehouse unit at the three pitches – two alongside each other lengthways at the far end of the building, each with a small spectator area, and a larger one closer to him, running the breadth of the warehouse with a spectator gallery down the length of one sideline. The pitches were laid with short, artificial, carpet-like grass, and the rectangular netted goals were fixed with backboards behind. Each pitch was enclosed by a five-foot wooden wall topped by a thick net curtain. Harsh electric lights flooded the playing areas to prevent shadows interfering with the football.

Paul approached the small reception desk below a screen showing the scores of the night's completed games and the games in progress. Brilliant! He booked in with the Centre manager, a dry and tetchy man of advanced years, and paid for the game, explaining it was the first one for the team.

'What are you calling yourselves?' asked the manager flatly, his pen perched over the match sheet.

'I-I don't know. We haven't discussed a name as such,' Paul stammered.

The manager sighed. 'I've got to put something down, or no one will know who you are.' He stared at Paul.

Gerry's rant earlier popped into Paul's head. 'Fat lads.'

'Fat lads?'

'Yeah . . . yeah, fat lads.' It needed something more. Paul thought quickly. 'All one word – capital F, capital L, then z and an exclamation mark at the end.'

'OK… like this?'

'Yeah, exactly like that. *The FatLadz!*'

*

As he waited for the others, Paul glanced at the games in progress. The ball moved fast on the short grass and tight control was critical to make and receive passes. There was all manner of players – old, young; fast, slow; good, not so good – and he was impressed by how organised some of the teams were. Thank goodness they had drawn the No-Hopers for the first match. It was important to get an early win to encourage the team and emphasise this whole thing was worth the effort.

He claimed one of the large round wooden tables between the café area and the pitches where the teams were congregating and stared across at the entrance. He wasn't convinced anyone would show. Then, twenty minutes before kick-off, Bobby arrived, with Bethan, Gav, Andy and Kev not far behind. They saw Paul and sauntered over, gazing around.

There was an awkward silence after initial greetings were out the way. They had never met up outside work before, except for the occasional leaving party, and that was just about the drinking. This was something more real, where they would have to work with each other and stand or fall as a unit.

With just over five minutes to go, Tiler wandered in and made his way through the tables to the group.

'Can't you *ever* arrive in good time?' Bobby Brown bellowed.

'He'll be late for his own funeral, that one!' added Bethan.

They paid their match fee and changed into their shirts. Paul realised he should have been more specific about kit. With Tiler particularly. He had changed into a washed-out blue dress shirt which may have fitted him twenty years ago; he'd torn the sleeves off unevenly like a poor man's imitation of an angry Hulk. Bethan wasn't much better in an old beaten-up Prison Service polo shirt. Andy was wearing a blue camouflage-patterned top, and Bobby Brown had on a tie-dyed grandad vest. And Kev? Well, he appeared to have chosen one of his wife's blouses. Only Paul and Gav were wearing anything resembling a football shirt.

'Let's get someone to take a picture in case we get into the National Newsletter,' said Kev.

Paul looked slowly around the table at his teammates, 'Maybe next ti—'

'FATLADZ TO PITCH NUMBER TWO. NO-HOPERS TO PITCH NUMBER TWO. FATLADZ AND NO-HOPERS TO PITCH NUMBER TWO.' The tannoy was loud enough for a building twice the size and so metallic, it set your teeth on edge.

'Here we go,' said Paul.

'Is that us? Fat lads?' shouted Kev. 'Is that the best you could do? Fat lads? Really?'

'Sorry, I was under pressure; it was the first thing I thought of – Gerry said it. Anyway, it applies to most of us! Tiler, put this on and start in goal. We can switch around as the game goes on.' Paul threw him the green shirt, which slipped through Tiler's hands and dropped to the floor. There was some shaking of heads, but Paul jumped in quickly. 'Remember what we've planned; we're lucky to have our first League match against the No-Hopers, but we need to conserve our energy 'cause we haven't trained yet. So, get a couple of goals, and then we sit back in defence and come out winning our first game. Bobby, you go sub and … Bobby? … Bobby?'

Bobby had already homed in on a female – the lady behind the counter serving refreshments. She was middle-aged – a few years older than him – and was slender and pretty with bleached-blonde hair and blue eyes. Chewing her gum, she seemed content to stand and listen to Bobby's chatter between customers.

'Bobby! Come back over here!' Paul shouted, feeling like the parent of a naughty child.

'What are you doing, you idiot? Can't you leave it alone?' Tiler added.

'Right. Bobby, you go sub, and we'll switch around as people tire.'

'Show time!' declared Tiler.

As they walked through the narrow entrance gate cut into the wooden wall, Paul's chest was fit to burst. This had really come together. Everyone was up for the game, and it would be something to interest the whole ROC – how the football team was doing. Others could join in once they saw it was an enjoyable distraction from work. They could really build a team and, more than that, encourage everyone to improve their health, even if they weren't involved with the football.

The referee announced two minutes of practice had begun. Paul tried to speak to him, but he was aloof, and when Paul suggested borrowing the match ball for practice, the ref picked it up and held it tightly under his arm. Paul noticed the No-Hopers had brought practice balls with them. He made a mental note, wishing they had done the same to give Tiler a feel for the ball and for everyone to get used to the pitch.

Then the whistle went for the captains to meet in the middle. There was a curt, almost hostile, shake of hands with his opposite number – a tall, blond, slender guy in his twenties. The referee spun the coin, and Paul called heads. It was tails, and the No-Hopers elected to kick off. As the opposing captain went to dispose of their practice balls, Paul tried to make a friend of the ref.

'We struck lucky having our first game against the No-Hopers, I think, Ref!'

'It's ironic,' the referee answered flatly.

'What is?'

'The name – it's ironic. It refers to their opposition.'

The referee put the ball on the centre spot and blew his whistle for kick-off. In those short seconds, Paul had a moment of realisation about the No-Hopers: their matching kit, their practice balls, their cool football trainers, not to mention six fit guys in their prime with working knees. But his epiphany was futile. Their captain passed the ball to a flyer coming through in the inside right channel, who ran unhindered to the goal area. He returned it to his captain following down the centre, who slotted it smartly past a dumbfounded, static Tiler. There was a sound like a gunshot as the ball hit the backboards, announcing the goal.

Paul looked around; no one had moved. All his team were in exactly the same positions as when they started – including himself. They were all glaring at Paul, and if looks could kill, he would surely be dead by now. The clock showed nine seconds. They were already one down. This did not bode well. Paul felt an idiot for being so blasé and expecting to just walk out and win the game. Now he'd be happy if they scored a single goal.

*

Paul looked around the table. Kev was rubbing his calf, making groaning noises similar to a ewe calling for its lamb, Tiler had his head face down on the table, and Bethan was staring into the middle distance. Andy had his head in his hands, while Gav and Bobby Brown were still gasping for breath.

The No-Hopers passed by on their way out.

'Thanks for the game, Ladz. Good effort,' one said with a snigger.

'Well done for trying – if you did!'

'Keep ya chins up – chins up – get it? They're *fat* lads – keep ya *chins* up, FatLadz!'

Paul was pleased to see none of his teammates responded to this sneering display of disrespect. So much for being humble in victory.

After a couple of minutes, Tiler lifted his head off the table. 'OK, I'll start, then.' He paused and took a deep breath. 'This has been the single most embarrassing and demeaning thing I've ever done in my life. And I've done some stuff. We should never have agreed to this – there's no one here like us. We're not fit, we're not that good at football and we've got no skill or stamina.'

'… or kit! We're a fucking laughingstock,' added Kev.

Paul stared at the wall while Tiler and Kev said their piece. But something inside him felt this *was* worth doing and it *could* be better. 'I agree, and it's my fault for underestimating the opposition, not realising how quick it all is, but we can do better. I expect every team struggles on its first game, but we're definitely not a laughingstock.'

'Are you The FatLadz!?' a scruffy teenager in a beige tracksuit shouted over Bobby Brown's shoulder. 'I do the scoreboard – I couldn't keep up! Every time I changed the score, they'd knock in another goal. I mean, twenty-three–nil; it was non-stop. I don't think anyone's ever scored that many before. I'm knackered!' He was still laughing as he walked away.

'You were saying?' said Kev.

'We're in for some shit when we get back to work,' said Andy. Bethan stirred. 'Don't tell them – or lie.'

'We can't lie. They've got a column in the *Echo* with all the scores and match reports,' said Andy, staring glassily at his phone. 'I've seen it.'

'It just gets better and better,' said Kev, shaking his head.

'Come on, guys. We can definitely do better. This is a challenge,' Paul said, clenching his fist. 'If it had been easy, it would have been pointless. Now we can make plans, get some training done, have a session together to work out how to play effectively, recruit some more players so we can have another sub. There's lots we can do to improve to build up to a win, whether that's next week or in ten weeks.'

Paul knew he had to work hard to instil some motivation now, or it would all be over. 'I know we're going to get some stick, but Rome wasn't built in a day. I thought we were going to be playing real no-hopers, but the referee told me they won the League *and* the Cup last year and are expected to do the same this year. My fault. My bad. Let's go home now and figure out how we can do better, and I'll try and organise a session. See if I can find someone who knows how to play. Extra players. Let's not give up straight away. What d'you think?'

Kev groaned into life, still rubbing his calf. 'I would have been much busier if it hadn't been for this going in the first half. I'm happy to carry on as long as I can get some treatment this week.'

Andy looked up from his phone. 'I'm too bulky for this – you've got to be tall and quick – but it was good to be playing in a team again, even a dysfunctional one. So, I'm still in 'til you find someone better.'

'It's not going to be easy recruiting more to play after this,' said Gav, 'and it didn't help the score that Tiler gave them four penalties!'

'That's a stupid fuckin' rule!' shouted Tiler immediately, clearly having been waiting for someone to have a go.

'Yeah, but it is the rule!' Gav hollered back. 'You're not allowed to step out of your area, and if you do, it's a penalty, and if you do it two times, it's two penalties, and if you do it four times, it's four fuckin' penalties. Even the ref couldn't believe it!'

'But if just one of you lazy fuckers had been covering back, I wouldn't have had to step outside – and I'll be stepping outside with you if you carry on, mate!'

'Come on, you two,' Bethan said. 'We all struggled out there, but we put in some passes, and Tiler made some good saves.' She sighed. 'They were just too strong for a first match. I'm definitely up for another go. I can get some players from the prison, if you want, Paul? My partner, Liz, would love to play.'

'I want to try and keep it in-house if we can, Beth – just the ROC. That's the whole point of it, really,' replied Paul.

'I'll make a twat of myself one more time, and if it's the same, I'm done,' said Kev.

Tiler groaned, rubbing his lower back. 'I'll think about it. We're in for such a bloody ragging in work.'

There was a thoughtful nodding of heads.

'Well, it is what it is, and we can only say what happened,' said Paul. 'Next week, we'll hopefully improve and move on from this. Maybe I can get some kit from somewhere, so we don't look such a mess. Be more of a team.'

If there was something you needed, from a bottle of designer perfume to a refurbed computer or a second-hand car, Gav was your go-to guy. He'd perked up by now. 'One of my mates is the team coach at the YMCA; he was telling me about their new sponsored kit. I'll find out what he's doing with the old one.'

'Brilliant,' said Paul. 'Let's keep this going. I'm sure we can do better with some experience. We've got Bisi-Bargains next week, and we definitely won't be distracted by the name this time!'

Bobby Brown was back up at the counter buying a Diet Coke and chatting with his new acquaintance. Paul shouted across to him, 'You up for another game next week, Bobby?' Bobby gave a thumbs-up, despite not having been involved in any of the conversation.

'That was simple,' said Paul.

'He's got his brains in his dick at the moment,' said Bethan.

Everyone laughed and the mood lightened.

'I'm on the morning shift,' said Paul, 'so I'll probably get all the stick. Anyone else?'

'Me,' said Andy, 'so we'll take it together.'

'Well, here endeth The FatLadz! Chapter One. Roll on Chapter Two. Dismissed!' said Paul.

There was a general stretching and rubbing of sore muscles as they eased themselves up. Paul smiled as he listened to them talking enthusiastically about the game and next week's fixture.

All except Bobby Brown; he was still talking and laughing at the counter with his newly acquired best friend.

*

Paul walked home full of beans. Yes, it was a ridiculous beating, but everyone appeared to enjoy meeting up and being a part of the team. Even Tiler, as much as he protested, wasn't totally against the idea of another game. After arriving home, he threw his kit in the wash and wandered into the sitting room where Paula was watching a David Attenborough programme.

She turned and smiled. 'You look happier. How did you get on?'

'Not great score-wise, but I think we made a lot of progress as a team, and it looks like we're going to carry on.'

'What was the score?'

'Twenty-three–nil.'

Paula gasped. 'If you're all still talking about another game, that *is* progress!'

'Yeah,' said Paul, glassy-eyed. 'Progress.'

*

Bethan was driving Gav, Andy and Kev home.

'I'm quite looking forward to the next game,' said Bethan. There were murmurs of agreement around the car. 'Not sure about keeping it in-house, though. I'm not sure we've got the depth, considering people aren't going to be available through the shift patterns and stuff.'

Kev nodded. 'Yeah, I suppose we all know a few possible players. Give it a chance and see if it takes off. But we can't keep going out there and being hit for this kind of score every week.'

'I'm only going to play until we either pack it in or you find someone slighter. This game isn't for someone my size,' said Andy. 'It's too difficult to turn.'

'They said that about the *Titanic*,' chimed Kev.

'Yeah, and look what happened to that!' Andy guffawed, and they all joined in.

When the laughter had died down, Andy said, 'Gav, have you got any cars? I put mine in for a service, and they gave it the last rites!' More laughter.

'Funny you should ask. I've got someone coming to the ROC on Friday about midday to have a look at a nice Yaris. If they don't take it, you're welcome to have a look. I'll be there 'til about six. Text before you come down.'

When Bethan started at the ROC, she'd been surprised when random people would turn up to buy random stuff from Gav. She'd heard that he'd sold books and paintings, (questionable) antiques, a dog (which everyone remembered disgracing itself on the operating floor), a horse (which everyone remembered disgracing itself in the car park), numerous cars, his father's motorhome and a fully equipped twin-axle catering unit. He'd explained he preferred the car park because his neighbours and his partner couldn't see what he was selling and how much he was making.

'Sounds great,' said Andy.

They were all getting out around the same area. 'Hey, Andy, good luck tomorrow morning with all the piss-takers,' shouted Bethan.

'Don't worry. They'll have a bit of this if they start,' Andy yelled, holding his huge fist in the air.

*

Chapter Four

It was only 6.10 in the morning, but there was uproar in the ROC.

'Say that again,' said Ahmed.

'Say what again?' Paul knew what Ahmed wanted.

'The score.'

'I already said it.'

'Yeah, but I think I've suddenly developed a hearing problem.'

'It was twenty-three–nil.'

'Twenty-three–nil?' Ahmed spluttered. Then, more slowly, 'twenty … three … nil?'

Even Carl was laughing. 'What the fuck? How long was the game? It must've been a couple of hours for them to score all those goals?'

'It wasn't,' said Paul.

'How long, then?'

'Ten minutes each way.'

'Ten minutes each way? Twenty minutes? Twenty-three goals in twenty minutes? Must've been like a fuckin' machine gun hitting the back of the net!'

Now everyone was laughing, even Paul and Andy who had steeled themselves for the inevitable.

Carl shouted over the cackling, 'I'll ask my nine-year-old daughter and her friends to play next week. They could do better than that!'

More laughter.

'Who was in goal?'

'Tiler.'

'Fuckin' Tiler? What the fuck?'

Carl said, 'What the fuck?' a lot.

Paul held up both palms. 'I know how it sounds, but it was really tough. We hadn't played together before, and the team we were playing won the League and the Cup last year. To his credit, Tiler made some good saves.'

'Kept you in the game, did he?' The laughter started again, with Ahmed holding his ribs.

Andy was having a busy time, but he managed to shout across, 'If you think it's that easy, you two come along and play. You're both invited!'

Paul nodded furiously. 'Everyone can join in. It's not exclusive, y'know.'

'I may just do that,' Ahmed said. 'Sounds like you need a bit of quality down there.'

'I certainly won't. I mean, what the fuck?' said Carl, then broke into fresh laughter.

All in all, the ribbing hadn't been too bad. Paul could handle a bit of good-natured banter, and on the plus side, he may have gained two new recruits.

Ahmed was slighter than most and handsome, with a mop of the deepest, darkest hair framing his small features. He was in his thirties and a good guy to have around. He was very practical, can-do, hands-on and an amazing car mechanic. This made him a popular colleague as he saved everyone a fortune. No job was too big for him, and he wouldn't take cash – always asking for something different. Sometimes very different!

Carl, though, could fly off the handle if provoked. Paul wasn't sure whether he'd be able to handle a match without causing a fight. However, beggars couldn't be choosers.

By six thirty, the ragging had settled down, and work had

taken over. Paul's workstation was quiet, so he checked through the roster to figure out who would be available for the following week's game – the difficult second game.

He found everyone would be available, except for Gav and Kev. He would try and replace them with … well, someone else. Then he'd arrange a training session beforehand – find someone who could teach them some tactics, then get on to Gav about the kit – loads to do. He was quite excited already; next week couldn't be worse than this week.

The slamming door made everyone jump. Paul knew that slam as well as everyone else. Some groaned; others sat at their desks and made themselves busy.

'For heaven's sake,' muttered Ahmed.

'Well? What happened?'

Paul did not want to speak to Gerry, so he kept it short.

'Well,' said Gerry over-dramatically. 'Well, well, well. What a pile of crap! Twenty-three–nil. Twenty-three–nil! I said you'd be fucking shit, and I was fucking right. Why did you bother turning up?'

Paul busied himself with paperwork, trying hard not to bite. He was OK with the good-natured barracking they'd got from the other guys, but this was downright malicious.

Gerry was in full flow. 'Did you lot actually go out onto the pitch? D'you know what? You're making this place a fucking laughingstock within the company – *and* with anyone who reads the *Echo* …'

As he was sounding off, Andy had risen angrily from his desk behind Gerry and was walking slowly towards him with his massive fist over Gerry's balding, pale scalp. Paul shook his head at Andy. 'It's not worth it!' he shouted, but Andy kept advancing.

'I know it's not fucking worth it,' Gerry was shouting at Paul, 'so do us all a favour, and pack the whole stupid idea in!'

Just as Andy's clenched fist was rising hammer-like over Gerry's head with Paul dreading the inevitable, Carl stepped across, took Andy's outstretched arm and turned him silently back to his desk. Paul let out a sigh of relief.

'I just hope the National Newsletter doesn't get hold of it.' Gerry slapped his cheek. 'Jesus, what will they think of me? All this shit could really affect any promotion for me, you know. If they think I'm behind it, what will they think of me?'

Paul finally bit. 'I think they know you wouldn't organise anything.'

'Damn right – 'cause d'you know what? When people organise charades like these, this is how they always turn out. All I want is for you lot to come to work and go home without fucking up. We don't need all this pissing about, so make that the last one. Bunch of piss-takers, for f …' Gerry's last words faded as he slammed the door even harder on the way out.

'One day I'm going to chuck him out the window,' said Andy over his shoulder.

'Why does he want to have a go at people all the time?' said Carl.

'Inferiority complex?' suggested Ahmed.

'I don't care,' said Paul. 'I've got this rolling now, so we're going to keep it going.'

'Put my name down for definite,' said Ahmed, 'even if only to upset that idiot!'

'And me,' said Carl. 'I'll make up the numbers when you're short.'

'Never mind that. You two are in the first team next week!' Smiling, Paul went back to planning the upcoming match.

*

Chapter Five

Friday arrived too soon. Paul had been unable to arrange a training session, but he had pencilled in everyone who could play on the following Monday, and the team was looking good. Ahmed and Carl were in, plus Bethan, Andy, Tiler, Bobby Brown and Paul himself. A half-decent bunch, surely.

Paul had spoken to each of them, and they had all started putting in some effort at training, albeit individually and at different levels. He had hoped to get everyone together, but personal commitments and work made that impossible. However, he was pleased the football had provided motivation for everyone to make some positive changes. He had even stopped smoking, started running and arranged a family gym membership. He was being particular about what he was eating and, although it was early days, he felt better mentally just knowing he was making an effort.

Bethan had said she was pleased to be out pounding the roads again. She told him she had been slacking these past couple of years as she was plummeting towards an easy contentment with Liz. This had given her a reason to get out and push through the pain, knowing she would do better on matchdays. She had told Paul that, with a little cohesion, they could do so much better as a team, and he could see this thought motivating her.

Andy kept repeating that his bulkiness was a huge disadvantage to the team, so Paul had spent some time trying to instil confidence into him. But Andy still maintained that Paul should get someone else if he wanted to win a match. Paul had tried to convince Andy to dig out his old army kit and get some training in to bolster his confidence. He was unsure whether he had succeeded.

Carl, yet to play, wasn't particularly tall, but he was twice as wide at the shoulder as at the waist. He always dressed in a tracksuit, as no other clothes would fit his muscular shape – nobody tried to get past him in a doorway, for sure! He was back on the weights, which was his equipment of choice in the gym. He still held the gym bench-press record, which no one had even come close to. Unfortunately, there were some questions asked after his success, and some called for a drugs test. Nothing was ever proven, but it left his record slightly tainted. He often talked about having another attempt and proving the rumours wrong.

Even Tiler, by no means a happy chappie, was out on the roads. Although running was too much for him, he could still work up to a fast walk and get his heart rate ticking over. On the Wednesday, Tiler had contacted the local running club and surprisingly enrolled on their upcoming Couch to 5K programme. Paul was a little worried about Tiler's heart, but he figured he wouldn't do it if there was a problem. He knew Tiler was determined to get some weight off, and this was his way of achieving it. It was another positive step, and everyone seemed on board.

Paul was pleased things were ticking away. Gav had been down to the YMCA. He'd enquired about the kit and, while he was there, he'd taken the opportunity to ask whether the coach would be interested in helping the Ladz with some tips, advice or general coaching. It was looking good for the kit, and he hadn't said no to the coaching, but neither before Monday, unfortunately.

Bobby Brown had rung Paul several times throughout the week, asking whether the game was going ahead. It was only when Paul had reassured him all was well that he showed any interest in the actual match. 'We're playing 'Bisi-Bargains' at seven thirty,' Paul told him each time, 'so make sure you're on time. OK?'

'Guaranteed,' returned Bobby. 'Looking forward to it!'

But Paul knew Bobby had a different motivation for turning up.

Kev had told Paul when they last spoke that he'd arranged treatment for his injured calf and was optimistic about recovering quickly. He lived close to Ahmed, and they were excited about putting a gym together in Kev's garage, but nothing was ever straightforward for Kev. Carl had rung Paul the previous night, asking if he'd heard the news.

'No. What?'

'Spoke to Kev. He got beaten up while walking his dog.'

'You're joking, right?'

'Wish I was. He was walking through the park with that labradoodle he bought a couple of months ago. You know what he called it, don't you?'

Paul remembered it was something stupid but couldn't recall what it was.

'No, go on.'

'Fatty. Fucking Fatty. I mean, what a prick he is sometimes!'

'Only sometimes? So, what happened?'

'Well, he's walking this bloody dog through the park, and it starts to wander off towards the river. It goes into the trees out of sight, and Kev's walking fifty yards behind, shouting, 'Fatty, Fatty! Come on, Fatty!' Unfortunately, a couple were sat on a bench, and the guy – a big guy – took exception, thinking Kev was shouting at him. This bloke gets up and, without any questions, whacks Kev right on the hooter. Kev's now walking round looking like a giant panda with a broken nose!'

As much as Paul tried not to laugh, it was too much, and soon the two of them were howling with laughter.

'Clown Kev strikes again!' Paul said, gasping.

*

Paul was on his break; he was still annoyed about Gerry's phone call the day before. 'Make sure you look at the newsletter when it comes out later. Something's in there that should interest you!' Gerry had said with a snigger.

'And what would that be?' Paul already had a good idea.

'Just read it. And I'll tell you what – I've put them right, in no uncertain terms!'

When it was published on the company intranet later that afternoon, the front page bore the subheading: *Who are these Fat Lads?* Paul clicked on the link. It was clear it wasn't going to be a positive article, as someone had thought it funny to put a photograph of an obese guy awkwardly trying to kick a ball into a goal.

The text below it read:

If you don't want to know the score – look away now! Yes, we now have our own football team to support and, believe me, they need all the support they can get! The guys and girls in the CROC have got together to play in the Six-a-Side Central League on a Monday night. The League organiser said after their first match that he had never seen anything like it. They really kept the scoreboard ticking over – but not in a good way!

Again, if you don't want to know the score – look away now! OK, sit down and ready yourself – it was 23–0! That big fat zero is for us – the Fat Lads! Thanks go to Gerry Spratt, ROC Manager, for letting us know. He also wanted us to know that he had nothing to do with it.

Good luck to the Fat Lads next week – they need it!

Paul was disappointed but not surprised. He'd suspected Gerry might pull a stunt like this, and he was worried it might dent what little morale the team had. If they could just get a win or even a competitive result, things would start to swing around.

The buzzer from the car park entrance brought him back into the room with a start. He answered the intercom. Through the camera, he could see a tall, scruffily dressed man, maybe early twenties, and unshaven with close-cropped hair. Paul thought twice about opening the gate and asked what he wanted.

'You selling a car?' the man yelled at the camera.

'Stay there!' Paul turned and shouted across the operating floor. 'Gav, it's for you. Go on; I'll keep an eye on this lot.'

'Thanks, Paul. I'll give you a cut!'

Paul rolled his eyes. They had all taken turns watching Gav's workstation so he could go and sell, well, whatever it was he was selling at the time. In return, he always bought the biscuits and newspapers for the following week.

Trev was on the next desk. During a quiet spell, he leaned over. 'Don't let that prick of a manager get to you, Paul.'

'I know. I just don't want us to give him more ammunition for next week, otherwise people are going to become despondent and start dropping out. It's on a knife edge already.'

'Maybe get a training session in next week. I hear the coach at the YMCA is going to help you out.'

'Gav's asked him, but I'm not sure yet. See how things go on Monday.'

'Who are you playing?'

'Bisi-Bargains ... but I'm definitely not pre-judging this one.'

'See if you can give them more than they "bargain" for!' Trev said. They both chuckled.

'That's terrible, Trev.'

Gav returned from the car park, waving a wad of notes. 'Not a bad day's work, if I say so myself!'

Paul rolled his eyes. 'Just another day in the life of Honest Gav!'

Chapter Six

Monday evening arrived in the blink of an eye. Paul had hoped to be more organised for the second game, but the training session he'd wanted to put together was proving elusive due to shift patterns and people's personal commitments.

He walked through the broad glass entrance into the cool air of the Football Centre, which was abuzz with conversation. Waves of players were coming and going between the pitches and the rest area, where preparations, post-mortems and recriminations were in loud discussion. All this was underpinned by the sounds from the football pitches: a deep thud from a shot on goal and sometimes the occasional crack as the ball hit the backboard and the subsequent cheers. The aromas of hot food and drink, the clinking of cutlery on crockery and the ear-splitting announcements over the tannoy all emphasised the vibrancy and energy within the complex.

Paul was loving it. He'd arrived half an hour early to soak up the pre-match atmosphere and to feed his joy of being involved in a physical pursuit again. He was buzzing with anticipation for the match and looking forward to seeing and playing alongside the 'Ladz'. Win or lose. What was that Shakespeare quote? 'If you can meet success and failure and treat them both the same…'

Good advice. Paul looked up at the scoreboard on his way past the counter. On the main pitch, the No-Hopers were 9–1 ahead against Football Crazies, no doubt heading for double digits soon.

A ball slammed against the backboards. There it was.

He saw an empty seven-seater table near the pitches and made a beeline for it across the crowded floor.

'Paul, Paul!' came a shout from the food counter. Even before Paul turned around, he realised … Bobby Brown. 'Over here! I've got us a table by the buffet!'

Paul looked across. Bobby had found a little recess next to the counter, where he was happily chatting to his new friend. Paul shook his head, grabbed Bobby's bag and marched to the table by the pitches. 'Never stops, never stops,' he said and sighed.

As Paul sat down, he reached for his phone to check for late withdrawals. Nothing. Great. So, a plan: Tiler in goal, Andy and Carl guarding at the back, him and Beth in the middle, and Bobby, who, whatever anybody thought of him, was quick and had an equally good shot on his left and right. Ahmed would start on the bench and go on for Andy, who would need a break after five or six minutes.

'Hi, Paul. We all set?' Bethan was standing next to a casually dressed, taller woman, whose long, loosely tied ponytail held her brown hair off her face, revealing her happy demeanour. 'This is my partner, Liz. If she can't play, she'll definitely watch.'

'Hi, Liz. Yeah, sorry 'bout that, but I just want it to be internal – y'know, workmates.'

'No problem,' Liz said with a grin. 'I'm looking forward to watching. It's the nearest thing we get to a night out these days.'

Bethan laughed. 'True!'

As the time ticked past, they all appeared – Tiler, late as usual, and Bobby Brown, dragged away from the food counter as usual. But Paul, still a little unsure about their commitment, was pleased everyone had shown. They still looked like a ragtag bunch compared to the other teams, who all had smart kits and, in some cases, were sponsored by their companies. That would never happen while Gerry was in charge.

Paul began his team talk. 'First of all, this is Beth's partner,

Liz.'

'Awesome,' said Ahmed. 'Our first spectator. Give it up for Liz!'

Liz laughed as they gave her an impromptu round of applause.

Paul moved on. 'Tiler, you did OK last week under fire. How d'you feel about staying in goal?'

'I was well and truly knackered after the last match, so I wouldn't even think about playing out. I was always a goalie, anyway.'

'Great. Andy, you and Carl patrol the back, me and Beth in the middle and Bobby up— Bobby, pay attention, for God's sake. You go up front. Ahmed, you start on the bench and come on to give Andy a break after five or six minutes, and then we'll wing it.'

There was general nodding around the table.

'We're playing Bisi-Bargains,' Paul continued, 'but we won't be reading anything into the name this week. We had a baptism of fire last week, but this time we'll play our own game, and I'm sure we can do better – no, we've got to do better – for ourselves.'

Unfortunately for Paul, that was the moment the No-Hopers walked past.

'Those fat lads are back for more!'

'Thought they'd have had enough last week.'

'I'm sure some of them look fatter!'

'A League record, I heard!'

They went off laughing and joking.

'What an obnoxious bunch,' Liz shouted after them, but they just laughed more.

'Anyway,' Paul said, 'play our own game, and ...'

'FATLADZ TO PITCH NUMBER ONE. BISI-BARGAINS TO PITCH NUMBER ONE. FATLADZ AND BISI-BARGAINS TO PITCH NUMBER ONE.'

'What the fuck?' shouted Carl. 'Couldn't they get louder speakers? They must have nicked those from Wembley or something!'

'Pitch One's the main pitch, so it's a bit bigger,' said Paul, 'We've got more room to move, but we're going to be more stretched and tired. Just try and keep it going. Think of that report in the newsletter last week.'

'We don't want that again, or to give Gerry a stick to beat us with,' agreed Andy.

'And Liz, you've got the whole spectator area to yourself.'

'Awesome,' she yelled over the buzz.

'Show time!' shouted Tiler.

Paul had had the foresight to pick up a ball from the garden for the two-minute practice. Ahmed had done the same so they could get a feel for the pitch and not go in completely cold.

The referee blew his whistle, and Paul approached the centre line. Bisi-Bargains – 'The Bisies', according to their logo – were well turned out in their fully sponsored yellow kit. This was in contrast to the Ladz, who looked as if they'd all called in at a charity shop on the way. Paul chose heads and won the toss; he decided to kick off.

'Right – places, everyone!'

Bobby Brown lined up alongside Paul, and the referee checked with the goalkeepers and blew his whistle to start the game.

Paul's first touch went to Bobby, who immediately passed the ball back to Bethan behind him, and then he turned and ran upfield. Bethan's head swivelled towards Andy, who had run straight up the right wing from right back, going past two defenders, and was now clear and free. She hit an inch-perfect pass straight onto Andy's right foot. Bobby had arrived at the back of the goal area, and Andy's first-time pass, as true as Bethan's, made it an easy tap-in for Bobby from behind the flailing goalkeeper.

The team went crazy – not just because it was their first goal, but they were winning the match, and they'd put together a great move which couldn't have been more perfect if they'd practised it! Amid high fives, fist pumps, Tiler whistling from his goal and Liz shouting from the stand, the Bisies stared in wonder at all the fuss.

Things eventually settled down, and the ref was able to restart the game. Paul was encouraging them all to maintain concentration so as not to immediately concede. Carl and Andy were doing amazing work at the back to thwart a vigorous onslaught, while Tiler was blocking any approach to the goal.

It was a clearance from Carl straight up the middle that enabled Paul, running diagonally from right to left, to get close to the goal area, but the keeper had come out to the edge of his box and left nothing to shoot at. Bobby was arriving to Paul's left and Beth to his right, and he could see the shadow of the first covering defender was taking Bobby's side, so Paul made a short pass off the outside of his right foot straight into Bethan's path. She slotted the ball sweetly into the bottom-right corner while the goalkeeper was still covering Paul.

More eruptions and even more noise from the stand as Liz went crazy over Bethan's effort.

'Well done, Ladz!' shouted Paul. It was going better than he'd ever dared hope. He took the opportunity to take Andy off as he was starting to cough. Paul took his place, and Ahmed went midfield with Beth. That was where the battle was fought for the rest of the first half – sometimes the Ladz getting the upper hand and sometimes the Bisies getting through – until the ref blew his whistle for the end of the first half.

They congregated down by the goal and congratulated each other on their performance.

'Well done, everyone,' shouted Paul above the noise. 'We're two ahead now, so we need to not only defend those goals but also keep them honest by attacking whenever we can, otherwise their whole team is going to plant themselves in our half, and we'll struggle to break through. Carl, got another couple of minutes in you?'

'Yes, boss, but probably not much longer than that.'

'OK. You stay on for a couple, and then Andy, you come back on for Carl, OK?'

Andy and Carl nodded, and the short break was over. After the

Bisies' kick-off, there was more haggling in the midfield as they tried to get through to Tiler, who had not had to make a serious save yet. Trying to relieve the pressure, Ahmed pushed a kick aimlessly up towards the left, and Bobby Brown spotted it. He broke past the last defender on the halfway line and got to the ball first. The defender managed to get back and position himself between Bobby and the goal, but when Bobby pulled the ball back, the defender's momentum took him too far and confused the goalkeeper. This opened up a tight gap to the right of the goal, and Bobby hit a solid right-footer that rattled in off the far post.

More applause and high fives for Bobby. Paul beamed. This was the best thing ever. Three–nil up – who would have believed it? Brilliant!

He made the change they had planned, and now they only had to hold out for another eight minutes. As the game progressed, he noticed the team, including himself, were slowing down. They weren't so quick to get into tackles and were backing off for too long. Bobby was staying back to help absorb the pressure. Then, the Bisies' shots started getting through. Tiler made a save to his low left but was only able to parry it; the ball went back out to an attacker, but Tiler was back up and blocking the left edge of the area to stop him shooting. To beat Tiler, the attacker played a slow pass across the front of the goal to another yellow shirt, who calmly slotted it towards the goal. Tiler was resolute he would not be beaten and dived full-length, managing to stop a certain goal.

There was applause all round as he stood with the ball, but he was fighting for breath and holding his chest.

Paul jogged across. 'You OK?'

'My heart's pounding like fuck,' Tiler gasped.

'Have a break. Don't worry; I'll get Carl back on.' He shouted, 'Sub, ref!'

Tiler was in no state to argue as he took off the green shirt and walked dejectedly over to Liz.

'You OK?' she asked.

'Yeah. Just totally unfit. Head's spinning – heart's pounding. Never been so unfit.'

'I'll go in goal,' said Paul. 'Carl, just do what you can to keep them out.'

'OK, boss,' replied Carl.

On restart, the Bisies immediately took charge of the ball. To the Ladz, it seemed like they were playing against ten men – the yellow shirts were everywhere. With some swift passing, they got their first goal. Bobby took the kick-off, but the halfway line was the closest that any of them got to the Bisies' goal for the rest of the match. The second goal came from some tired defending as Andy and Carl tried to move their vast bulks around the pitch. Paul was doing his best, but they were shooting at will now, and all he could do was watch as the third goal hit the backboard. His defence, for what it was worth, was compressed to within a few yards of the area, trying to block each shot to keep the match at a draw and get their first league point.

Then the Bisies scored their fourth. Paul had made a diving save, but the rebound went straight to their main man who didn't miss. Even Bethan had her hands on her knees, trying to get her breath back.

With forty-five seconds to go, Paul tried to rally the troops. 'Come on, guys, one final push. Don't give in.'

As much as they tried, there was nothing left in the tank, and the Bisies' fifth goal went in with seconds to go. Mercifully, there was no time to restart as the whole team was spent. They traipsed back to their table.

Tiler and Liz left them panting in their seats to go for more water. They returned to an unexpectedly buoyant table as Paul congratulated them on their efforts. 'Well done, everyone; so much better than last week. We really showed some skills out there tonight.'

Liz agreed. 'You all did really well. The first-half efforts show you've all got the ability, but the fitness is letting you down bigtime.'

There were nods around the table. Carl nudged Paul and nodded towards the pitch. The Bisies were walking in their direction.

'Here we go again,' said Paul.

Everyone's head turned, waiting for the barbs and insults.

'Well done, guys – great game,' their captain said. 'Your fitness let you down in the end, but a brilliant effort for only your second match.'

'Thanks,' replied Andy. 'We were just saying it was a massive struggle by the end.'

'We thought you were going to run away with it after that first half. We were exactly the same as you a year ago, but by playing regularly and training, it does get better.'

'Thanks for the advice,' said Carl. 'We thought you were coming over to take the piss like the team we had last week.'

'Oh no, man. Who did you play?'

'The No-Hopers,' interjected Ahmed, still disgruntled.

'That bunch of obnoxious pricks,' said the captain, as the rest of his team shook their heads. 'None of the other teams bother with them. They shouldn't even be in our league – they keep refusing promotion because they like to win. They say they can't play on any other night, so we're stuck with them. They win every game and take the piss, then they win the League Competition and, most annoying, the Cup.'

'Infuriating,' said Paul.

'Yeah. They know there are sides in the next league who would take them apart, so they won't go. They're shit-scared. But you'll find the rest of the teams are either friends or workmates, like us, who just want to meet up, stay fit and have a good game of football.'

'That's exactly what we want,' said Andy.

'Thanks for the game. We'll catch up with you through the season,' the captain said.

The teams shook hands and fist bumped as the Bisies passed by.

'That was unexpected,' said Bethan. 'Goes to show what a bunch of arseholes that lot were last week.'

'Absolute arseholes,' agreed Paul.

'Ya lives an' ya loyns,' mumbled Tiler in a faux-Chicago accent.

Bethan laughed. 'Ya do!'

Bobby Brown had disappeared to the buffet bar, deep in conversation over his customary Diet Coke. His body language made it clear that if their relationship hadn't yet progressed, it was about to. He was a quick worker, for sure.

'It's disgusting,' said Bethan, folding her arms.

'Why? Why shouldn't he chat her up?' asked Carl.

'He started last week,' she replied. 'Trouble is, he's got a wife and two kids at home – two little girls.'

'Oh, yeah, of course. That is bad, really bad.'

Paul averted his eyes to carry on with the debrief. 'As the Bisies said, brilliant first half; couldn't have gone better. Three–nil up at one stage. Andy and Carl, absolutely solid at the back. Beth, Ahmed, some lovely touches, and a brilliant goal, Beth. Tiler, some great saves. I think you're going to get better with every match …'

'… you fat twat,' added Carl.

'Fuck off, Carl!' replied Tiler.

Everyone smiled.

But Carl didn't let it go. 'That save,' he said. 'Did you dive, or did you fall?' More laughter. 'Last week after the game, Tiler was so depressed, he went out and threw himself in front of a bus – the bus went under him!' Now everyone was laughing hard. 'They used to call him Dracula – 'cause he was afraid of crosses!'

'I nearly fell out of my pram the first time I heard those old jokes, arsehole!' shouted Tiler over the laughter.

Paul persevered. 'And Bobby,'—Bobby wasn't even in earshot—'if we can get the ball to him, he's shown he can score.'

'He's shown us that, all right,' Carl said, flicking his thumb towards Bobby at the bar.

Paul pretended he hadn't been interrupted. 'We all heard what the Bisies said, that they were worried until our fitness let us down, so that's what we've got to work on. We can all do it at our own level. Just do what you can, and we'll be able to keep scoring goals until the end. We may even get as far as winning a match!'

Everyone nodded, eyes and smiles wide.

'I noticed on the sheets we've got a Cup match next Monday,' Paul continued, 'so let's target that. We'll up our fitness, and in the meantime, I'll sort out a team. Anyone else want to say something?'

Andy perked up. 'I just want to say that it's great playing for a team again. We don't get much encouragement in work, that's for sure, but I think we all worked for each other tonight; we climbed up together, and we went down together. That's teamwork.'

There were general sounds of agreement and 'hear, hear' around the table.

'Nice one, Andy. Quite right,' said Paul. 'Anyone else?'

'I think we should thank Liz for being our first spectator,' suggested Ahmed.

Everyone agreed and thanked her.

'I'm proud to have filled that role,' she said with a laugh and a mock bow.

'If that's all … Everyone, dismissed,' announced Paul.

They started chattering amongst themselves, but, as they'd had a late start time, the place was emptying.

As they were walking away, Tiler shouted across to the buffet bar, 'Oi, Romeo! Don't forget your bag!'

Bobby Brown turned around sharply and was about to shout something in return, when he obviously thought the better of it and simply nodded. Paul chuckled quietly to himself, as did the rest of the team.

*

When Paul arrived home from the football, he was smiling broadly. Paula said, 'Wow! You had a win tonight?'

'Ha, no, but we started to gel. We even had a spectator.'

'Really? Who?'

'Liz, Bethan's partner.'

'Great! Perhaps I'll bring the boys down next week.'

'It's a good vibe there; I think they'd enjoy it. The team's really coming together. With a few more players, we might even go on to win a match!'

He made some tea and began a checklist:

Enquire about the Cup match

Ask Gav about the kit

Organise a training session

Make a team WhatsApp group

Find a coach/trainer

He set up the WhatsApp group immediately and included anyone who had played or was interested in playing, so they could easily communicate. Then he went to bed – happy with his evening's work.

*

Chapter Seven

Bethan was by the kettle with Trev. Her legs were aching, but she was still buzzing. 'How did it go last night, Beth?' Trev asked. She and Bobby Brown were the only ones on the day shift who had played the night before.

'Really good,' she replied. 'We lost five–three but got the feeling we were starting to gel. We were three–nil up at one stage and had them running, but we couldn't maintain it. It was like running through treacle, and they were scoring at will by the end. We were shattered, I mean, completely – all of us. Tiler had to go off and Paul finished in goal.'

'Looks like I missed a good game.'

'Yeah. They were a nice group of guys, too, and came over for a chat after the match.'

'Nicer than the No-Hopers, then?' Trev said.

'Totally! They thought we were going to run away with it in the second half, but they could see we'd lost it when we stopped chasing. Put us right about those bastards we played last week, that's for sure. Apparently, they've got the same attitude with everyone, and all the other teams detest them. But it was a good night, and if we can sort out our fitness, we might even win a game.' She noticed Trev look down. 'You still miss it?'

'Yeah. It never goes away, even after all these years. I'd love to be out there with you guys, but one bad turn on this ankle'—still looking down, he extended the offending leg—'and I'm screwed.' He paused then lifted his head. 'I'm really pleased for you all, though. It sounds like it might take off after all.'

Bobby Brown wandered in and flicked a teabag into his mug.

'How did you get on last night, Bobby?' asked Trev.

A thoughtful smile spread across Bobby's face as he poured hot water over the teabag.

'He means the football,' Bethan said with a scowl.

'Oh, yeah. The football …'

'We lost five–three, and you scored two of the goals … remember?' she pressed him.

'Ah, yeah. Good game, good game.' He grabbed the milk from the fridge and poured a dash into his mug. Bethan was glaring at Bobby, who exited sharpish, leaving the milk on the side.

'What was that about?' Trev asked.

'He's at it again, screwing around. Honestly, so blatant – no shame. I mean – his wife – those poor girls.'

Trev silently shook his head. 'Paul's doing a good job, getting you all together, particularly as some don't get on.'

'Ha, yeah, he's managing to keep a lid on it, although Tiler's always having a go at Gav and Carl; they've always got something to say to each other. We've got a Cup match next week, so await events – see if I make the team!'

*

On returning, Bethan checked the newsletter which had just been published on the intranet. The editor had rung the ROC in the morning to find out what had happened in the football. Bethan had taken the call. He sounded disappointed that the team had done so well and said a 5–3 loss was not headline news, unlike the previous week's score. But she pushed him hard to include something about the match, as the team were on a high after a close game and had achieved the close scoreline after only one

previous game. He said he would mention the match. And he did:
RAILFAIL:
THE FAT LADS CONTINUE THEIR LOSING STREAK!
'What?' she gasped, clicking on the headline.
Yes, the Fat Lads are still struggling to get into any kind of form and went down to a dismal defeat against inferior opposition last night. Unable to get a foothold in the game, they were well beaten by a procession of goals in the second half, while their spectator(!) watched from the sideline. Next game: next Monday. Tickets selling fast! (Lol!)

'For fuck's sake. Look at this crap, Bobby.'

'What is it?'

'I spoke to that prick this morning. He was as nice as pie, really interested, and then he goes and writes something like this!'

Bobby and Trev read it over her shoulder.

'What a piece of crap!' said Bobby.

'Unbelievable,' agreed Trev.

'I'm gonna ring him now and tear the shit out of him. What a twat! I'll give him …'

'Whoa, hold on a minute, Beth,' said Trev, ever the peacemaker. 'Don't bite. That's exactly the reaction those types want. Just bide your time or you'll end up on a disciplinary, not to mention giving ammo to Gerry.'

'Someone mention my name?' Gerry said, walking into view.

'Ah, for f—' Bobby didn't finish the sentence, and they all walked back to their desks.

'Good write-up in the rag mag for you lot again. Ha, "Railfail"! I wonder who came up with that!'

Bethan had a sneaking suspicion who that might have been. It made sense that the editor would have rung Gerry before publishing a report; it looked like he was in Gerry's pocket. Annoying. Paul was coming in for the night shift, so she decided to tell him of the conspiracy to belittle what they were trying so hard to achieve.

Nobody spoke to Gerry except to respond to work-related

questions. As much as he tried to start an argument, or disrespect and insult them, nobody bit.

Bethan sighed with relief when he eventually left. 'Gerry Spratt. What a nice guy … said nobody ever!'

Chapter Eight

Bethan had finished her shift and was ready to leave when Paul arrived. She filled him in on the day's action and handed over. 'Oh – and that fucking idiot stuck his oar in again.'

'What's he done now?' Paul didn't need to ask who she was talking about.

'Look at this; I printed it out.'

He read the report.

Bethan explained she had spoken to the editor, and he had seemed quite interested. 'He was a bit disappointed we didn't lose by twenty goals again, but he said he'd put something in. Then he wrote that pile of shite. And *then,* that prick came up here and made it quite clear he'd had a hand in it. He was particularly proud of "Railfail".'

Paul was shaking his head. 'What *is* the matter with the man? And the editor; you'd think the company would give us some support, even if our brain-dead line manager won't.'

'I was going to ring the editor this afternoon and give him a right royal roasting, but Trev said I shouldn't.'

'Probably for the best – keep you in a job, eh, Beth?' She smiled. 'We're on our own,' Paul continued, 'so let's get stuck in and enjoy it. Anyway, we're all in a WhatsApp group now, so we can communicate and support each other. Should be a good lau—'

'My God! Look at the state of you!' shrieked Bethan, looking past Paul's shoulder.

Paul turned round. Coming round the corner for his first shift back after his incident in the park was Kev, with panda eyes and a bent nose.

'Don't start, Bethan. It still hurts like fuck.'

Gav was also arriving for the night shift. 'Fair play; you don't do things by halves, do you, Kev? Did you change the dog's name yet?'

'Piss off!'

'Are you telling me to piss off, or is that the dog's new name?'

'Fuck you!'

'Even worse!' Gav shouted over everyone's laughter.

'Look, I just want a quiet night tonight – no hassle and no problems, OK?'

'Not OK,' said Trev. 'You've got a shedload of engineering work tonight – definitely not the best night to come back.'

'Bollocks,' said Kev with feeling.

'Gav,' said Paul, 'can you chase up that kit this week? It would be great if we could all turn up in matching gear – worth a couple of goals per game, I reckon.'

'No probs. I'll go over and see him on Thursday; find out the score with some coaching, too.'

'Great job. Thanks.'

The intern had also just arrived. 'Who am I with tonight?' he asked.

'Not me!' replied Kev.

'Come with me,' Gav said. 'You won't learn anything from that prick, anyway.'

*

The end of the week soon came, and Paul was at home, looking forward to sorting out the team for the Cup match.

Gav had posted a bit of interesting news on WhatsApp: apparently, the intern played a bit of football and, if required, would be pleased to step in. This would help with the weekly team changes due to the shift work.

Paul had asked if anyone knew his name, but nobody answered. *I'll put him down as 'Intern' for now*, he'd texted.

The more players he had, the better the team would do, as he really wanted to have two substitutes for each game to cut down on tiredness. He wrote down the current list of players:

Ahmed
Andy
Bethan
Bobby Brown
Carl
Gav
Kev
Intern
Paul
Tiler (Goalkeeper)

He read and re-read the following week's roster to fit in the people who were available – nobody had said they were unavailable for other reasons:

Tiler (Goalkeeper)
Paul
Bethan
Gav
Intern
Kev
Ahmed

No Bobby Brown, though. It was a blow not to have him for this match – with good service from the rest of the team, he could score at will. No Carl or Andy, who were so useful at the back. Never mind; they could work with what they had.

It was deathly quiet in his study above the dining room, so he almost jumped off his seat when his phone rang. It was the Central League organiser.

'You *are* the manager of The FatLadz! aren't you?' he asked.

'Well, "manager" might be a bit strong, but go on …'

'There's a change of plan, I'm afraid,' he said. 'The DrunkSkunks can't raise a team for the Cup match on Monday, as some of them are working away. The good news is that they've forfeited the game, so you're automatically through to the second round. Congratulations. The bad news is you no longer have a game on Monday; you'll be back in for your League match a week Monday.'

'Great news about the Cup,' Paul said slowly, thinking fast. 'If we're not playing, could we hire a pitch for an hour on Monday to do a training session?'

'Teams sometimes do that, but you'd have to speak to the Centre manager, and it would have to be before the games begin. Give him a ring tomorrow.'

'Thanks, will do.'

Paul hung up thoughtfully. This was good news on two counts. One, obviously, that they were through to the second round of the Cup, and two, they had the chance to get this elusive training session in. Paul made the announcement on the WhatsApp group, and it wasn't long before the first emojis started arriving; everyone was pleased and up for the training session. Paul figured that if he could organise it early enough, everyone would be able to make it.

He also had a thought. Why was he asking a coach from another team for his help, when right in front of him was someone who had been heavily involved in football, albeit a while ago? He decided that whatever the YMCA coach said, he would ask Trev if he'd be prepared to pass on some of his knowledge. That would keep it in the family, so to speak.

Paul put a cross through his team sheet, threw it in the bin and rejigged his to-do list:

Ring the Centre manager

Remind Gav about the kit

Organise a session

Find a coach/trainer – hopefully Trev

*

The following morning, there was a group post from Gav:

Good news and bad news. Got the kit, so we'll look the biz in future. Bad news is the coach doesn't have enough time to take anything else on. He wished us luck, though.

Paul rang the Centre manager immediately to organise a pitch for Monday. The man was very accommodating, even offering to come in early so they could get the full hour. All Paul had to do now was call in at work to speak to Trev, who was on the day shift. Great – things were coming together nicely.

He headed for the ROC straight away. When he arrived, Daniel was cooking breakfast. 'Oh, my God,' said Paul as he walked past the breakout area.

'Yes?' said Daniel.

Paul laughed. 'Any spare?'

'Sorry, bare minimum today. I may be God to you, but I still can't do that loaves-and-fishes thing.'

'Doh!'

Paul continued to the operating floor. Trev was explaining the evolution of the signalling system to the intern.

'Hi, Trev,' said Paul.

Trev raised his eyebrows. 'You're not in today, Paul.'

'Just popped by for a word.'

'Is it private?'

'No, no. It's about the footy.'

'You're not going to ask me to play, are you?'

'Lol. That'd be brilliant.' Paul smiled sympathetically. 'But in the meantime, how do you fancy doing some coaching for us? I've organised a session at the Centre on Monday at four thirty. It would be fantastic if you could come down and pass on some of your knowledge and give us some structure. What d'you think?'

'I don't know, Paul. I've been out of the game so long. I tried to keep up with all the new stuff – training regimes, schedules, stretches and exercises – but it got too depressing, if I'm honest.'

'I can understand that, but you still know more than any of us,' said Paul. 'Just give us some tips on things like ball retention, when to pass, when to shoot, marking and positioning. You'd probably enjoy it.'

'I don't get much pleasure out of watching others doing the very thing I'd like to be doing.'

'Wouldn't you get some pleasure out of seeing a team you coached win a match?'

'Maybe. Let me sleep on it.'

'Of course. I'll give you a ring tomorrow.' Paul's heart sank. He could understand why Trev might feel coaching would be depressing, but even so, he'd thought Trev would bite his hand off. However, once again, Rome wasn't built in a day. He'd ring him tomorrow – Saturday.

Daniel was bringing in the breakfasts, and the smell in the room was amazing. Paul turned to the management and technical training intern. 'If you carry on indulging, you'll end up bigger than us!'

'I just can't say no to these amazing breakfasts – this is restaurant-quality food. And last week Daniel did us a curry for dinner. I mean, just wow!'

'We're lucky to have him. One of the guys said you might be interested in a game with us down at the Centre?'

'I haven't played properly since school, but, yeah, I wouldn't mind. I love kicking a ball around.'

'Great. Come down to the Centre next Monday, four thirty. We can do a bit of training. Should be fun.'

'I'll be there. Got nothing planned.'

'Awesome. See you then, then!'

Paul's stomach growled. The sight and smell of the breakfasts was making his mouth water. Everyone laughed when he shouted, 'I can't stand this any longer. I've got to get out of here!'

He headed for the exit, in search of a full English.

Chapter Nine

Paul was walking towards the Football Centre. He was looking forward to the training session, particularly as Trev had rung him on Saturday morning to say he'd be there. They'd have someone to run the session now, rather than everyone running round like headless chickens.

He met Kev and Ahmed in the car park. 'All set?'

'Yeah, bring it on,' said Ahmed. 'This is what we're doing all this gym work for.'

The Centre's bright lights showed the patches around Kev's eyes were finally starting to clear. 'How's the old face doing, Kev? Getting back to normal?' Paul asked.

'D'you know,' Kev replied, 'I reckon I've heard every black eye joke a hundred times over the past couple of weeks. I don't know what people would've talked about if it wasn't for me!' He raised his eyes to the ceiling. 'Anyway, it gave people a laugh.'

Giving others a laugh was high on Kev's agenda, even if it was at his own expense. It made him happy to crack jokes or prank people to get a reaction. Apparently, his nickname of Clown Kev had started in school then followed him through each job to his current position. But he was OK with it, as long as it cheered people up.

Paul went straight to the desk to pay the Centre manager, who had put them on the main pitch and provided a bag of old footballs and a stack of space markers. Perfect.

When he turned round, he stepped back with a start. Andy had arrived and was standing next to him. 'How do you do that?' asked Paul.

'What?' replied Andy, his brow knitting together.

Paul just shook his head. Bethan was walking over to them, and the others had begun to arrive. Carl and Trev were with Gav, who was carrying the new kit; they were followed by the intern and Bobby Brown. Bobby was not alone. He waltzed into the Centre, not exactly arm-in-arm with his new lady friend – Stella – but as close as possible.

'This is really starting to piss me off,' Bethan said to Andy and Paul. 'Why can't he leave it alone for once? He's using us as cover – an alibi. Such a shit.'

Paul didn't comment. No point provoking Bethan further. He, Andy and Bethan joined the others.

Gav had grabbed a table and lifted the heavy kitbag onto it. He started to arrange it all neatly. 'This is only to borrow for now, so everyone has got to take care of their own stuff and return it at the end of the season,' he said defensively. 'There's different sizes – thirteen complete kits plus goalkeeper, wherever that lazy fucker is. There should be something for everyone. So be careful and look after it.'

It wasn't long before the tabletop was looking like a Primark clothes shelf in the January sales.

'What the hell are you lot doing?' said Gav. 'By the time I tidy this lot, the hour'll be over! For fuck's sake!'

'Oi, oi, saveloy! Where's mine?' Tiler had arrived.

'Better late than never,' said Kev.

'I would have preferred never,' said Gav. 'There, look, gloves as well. Now perhaps you'll save one!'

'Up yours, Gavin,' was Tiler's considered reply.

Once the kit was sorted and consigned to individual kitbags, Paul got down to business. 'Trev is here to take the session, so do what he says and take on board any tips and tactics. Also, you may notice we have our management and technical training intern this evening as a new starter—'

'I don't even know your name,' said Kev, helping Gav tie up the kitbag.

'Call him what I call him,' interrupted Tiler.

'What's that?'

'Well, he's the management and technical training intern – it's got to be MATTI!'

Everybody laughed as Matti slowly shook his head. 'Call me what you like,' he replied. 'Matti is definitely better than some of the things I've been called!'

Paul clapped his hands. 'Can we get on here?'

'Yeah, come on,' Trev said. 'Bring the balls. Everyone in!'

*

Paul was relieved that Trev opened with some stretching and warm-up exercises – he didn't want any injuries from just a training session. He was quite pleased with the way everyone held up, and in ten minutes, they were all warm and ready.

'First of all, everyone listen!' Trev began. 'You're going to do all the drills for five minutes per drill. Because we don't have that much time, we'll do a three-drill circuit twice and then finish with a match. All good?'

Everyone nodded and mumbled agreement.

'Tiler, you go in goal. Bobby and Andy, grab a ball and go down with him – take shots – start small, just a couple of yards straight at him – warm up slowly, gradually moving away 'til you're hitting good shots – nothing ridiculous. It's about building confidence and Tiler knowing his limitations after not doing this for so long.

'Beth, Gav and Matti, I'm going to put some markers down, and you can practise dribbling and turning. Six markers, zigzag on the way out, sprint straight back, next person.

'Paul, Ahmed and Kev. We'll set out a running lane, around twenty-five yards. Take turns and run how I tell you – it might be sprint or sideways or backwards, then jog back for the next person. Any questions?'

They set about their tasks enthusiastically, practising shooting, passing and defending, as Trev gave them tips on where to be and how to build an attack. Tiler stayed in goal all the time; he said he was enjoying being back between the sticks, or in Gav's words, 'the lazy fat bastard couldn't manage the runs.' Paul could see that Matti was going to be an asset to the team as he was sharp and energetic.

Although the drills were demanding, they all enjoyed them, then they played a short match for the last fifteen minutes.

They left the pitch promptly and returned the equipment to the office before going back to the table for a debrief. They collapsed onto their chairs with their water bottles and towels, ready to go over the session. All except for Bobby Brown. He had walked past the table and was heading for the buffet area.

'Bobby, can we have five minutes of your time? Just five minutes,' called Paul.

'I'm just getting a drink – half a minute, and I'll be there.'

'Tell 'im 'e's dropped, boss!' shouted Gav, loud enough to make Bobby look back.

'I think it went really well today,' said Paul. 'What do you reckon, Trev?'

'Yeah. Well done, everyone. You all stuck at it. I could see you were getting more confident on the ball as we progressed. So much better than trying to learn during a match.'

Bobby joined them.

'This training session has been invaluable,' Trev continued. 'I've enjoyed it, even if my ankle is as sore as hell!'

The others shot him sympathetic smiles and thanked him for his help.

'Definitely worth it, though – great to kick a football again,' he said.

Paul took over. 'Yeah – thanks, Trev. With all the players we've now got and the tactical coaching from Trev, I feel we can compete and maybe even win a match at some stage. But it still depends on who's available at any one time. We can mix and match each game; I just want to win one before the end of the season. That would be amazing. It's a pity we've got to wait a week before we put all this into action, but it'll give us time to take it in. Stick with your own training, whatever that might be, and I'm sure we'll see a difference next week. Anyone else want to say anything?'

'Yeah,' boomed Tiler. 'Tell Gavin to stop poncing round like a fairy, and we could have more of a chance of a wi—'

'Fuck you, you fat cu—'

'Pack it in, you two!' hissed Bethan. 'There's kids round here now, so watch your language, or you'll get us all chucked out!'

'Anyway, my name's Gav, not Gavin.'

Tiler just couldn't help himself when Gav was around. 'No probs, *Gavin*.'

Paul tried again. 'Anyone with anything *sensible* to say?'

'Just quickly,' said Ahmed. 'I can see now it wasn't just the fitness that let us down in the last match, it was also tactical naivety.'

'Say what?' said Kev and Carl in unison.

'Tactical naivety – we didn't know what we were doing. It would be great if Trev came down and watched; he could coach us as we went along.'

They all thought it was a good idea, and Trev was on board too. 'It'll be nice to be involved again,' he said.

'Brilliant,' said Paul. 'So, if there's nothing else, roll on Monday. Dismissed!'

The Centre was starting to liven up as other teams were arriving for their Cup matches. Paul had a pang of envy. He announced he'd hang around for a while to watch some games and was pleased that everyone, except those on the night shift, were staying too. Bobby Brown had his own agenda.

As they walked back to the pitches, they bumped into the Bisi-

Bargains boys. 'Hey, FatLadz! Who are you playing tonight?'

'We got a bye, so no game for us,' Paul replied. 'We took advantage, though, and had a training session. It was good. Yourselves?'

'No-Hopers. Can't believe it. First round too. Gutted.'

'Well, give it your best shot – we'll come over and watch. Good luck, guys.'

'Cheers.'

As they headed to the main pitch, the No-Hopers were making their entrance through the clear glass doors. They breezed through the tables as others made way for them, but there was no mutual acknowledgement; nobody spoke to them, and they spoke to no one. Their matching red-and-gold tracksuits had their names embroidered on the lapels, above a predatory bird of some kind. They settled at a table away from the other teams, isolating themselves.

'Who the fuck do they think they are?' spat Tiler.

Paul noticed something strange about them but couldn't put his finger on it.

During their match, the Bisies tried their best, but the outcome was much as expected. The No-Hopers – sharp, well-drilled, fit and deadly accurate – against a bunch of mates out for a good game of football; there was always only going to be one result. At the end, the No-Hopers offered no words or handshakes as they swept back to their table, their job done. Paul noticed they didn't even congratulate each other. Odd.

After commiserating with the Bisies, the Ladz all stayed for the next match. LadyKillers, an all-female team, were up against the SharpShooters. Both teams had good support, and the game didn't disappoint. First one way, then the other, the evenly matched teams struggled to score, and it took extra time to decide the result. The nippy Killers were too fast and fit for the Shooters, and in the end they ran away with it.

'Either one of those teams would be a tough game, Paul,' said Andy.

'Definitely. They're not drawing the next round until this one is over. Hopefully, all the games will be completed tonight.'

Once the action was over, they slowly disbanded and headed home. Nobody bothered saying goodbye to Bobby Brown, who, needless to say, was still at the counter. They'd had a good evening of football and were looking forward to their next game.

'Hey, Gav,' Andy shouted as they all parted, 'I still haven't had a car. Keep an eye out.'

'I am – should have a BM in at the end of the week, a black one. The guy's having a Jet Ski off me for it. I'll let you know for definite.'

'A fuckin' Jet Ski?' said Tiler. 'Is there nothing he doesn't deal in?'

Chapter Ten

Friday came round again fast, and Paul was back in work after a couple of days off. It was a struggle to get up at five o'clock, but he was there in plenty of time, much to the appreciation of Dudley, who had worked the night shift.

Gwynfor, one of the older members of staff who had given up working overtime as he approached his retirement, wasn't so lucky – he was waiting for Tiler. A devout Welsh Baptist and the most relaxed person you would ever be likely to meet, Gwynfor became a different animal when he was being relieved by Tiler. By 5.50 he was pacing the floor; by 5.55 he was doing the same with his bag on his back and his keys in his hand.

Tiler walked round the screens as the clock ticked over to six.

'Fucking unbelievable!' shouted Gwynfor. 'Every fucking time!' (Gwynfor was a stickler for pronunciation.)

'What?' said Tiler with false innocence.

'One more second, and you would have been late. You are absolutely fucking useless, do you know that, boyo?'

Paul and Ahmed kept out of it. Tiler's timekeeping annoyed everyone, but Gwynfor took exception more than anyone.

'I wasn't late, though, was I? And'—Tiler paused for effect— 'I only get paid from six o'clock. So …' He shrugged, palms up.

Gwynfor quickly went through the night shift with Tiler and readied to leave. 'There you are, boy. I'm late going home now.

Thanks for that!'

'Well, book the soddin' overtime if you're that cut up about it!' countered Tiler.

'I probably won't get to sleep now after this upset. Every time. Every time! Fed up of it, I am.' The last words were uttered as he walked around the corner, slamming the door behind him Gerry-style.

'You know it winds him up, Tiler. Why d'you do it?' said Ahmed.

'Whatever. He'll get over it.'

*

As the day moved on, Paul started looking through the WhatsApp messages. The gist of them was everyone enjoyed the session and was hoping to be available for the next match against the Bankers.

Paul grabbed the new roster off the wall and began to assess who was available Monday evening. None of the team had told him they were otherwise unavailable, so that made it easier. The only night-shift workers were Gav and Ahmed, so that gave him Tiler, Carl, Andy, Bethan, Bobby Brown, Clown Kev, Matti and himself, which meant two subs. All the teams seemed to use two subs, so Paul was pleased to comply, particularly in these early games. Trev wasn't working either; hopefully he would be there too.

So, things were looking good for Monday. What's more, they'd had their training session, they had their new kit, and everyone was pounding the roads or the weights in search of extra fitness. For Paul, this was what it was all about. Even though they were only a couple of games in, there was a keenness and a camaraderie in the ROC that certainly hadn't existed before. Even those not involved were talking about the football and the team's progress. Paul, although optimistic for Monday's game, did not have any preconceptions. Those had been kicked out of him by the No-Hopers. They just had to go out, enjoy the game and try their best.

Tiler was improving every time he touched the ball, and the others were starting to have some faith in him. Andy and Carl were solid but tired quickly. Bethan and Bobby would run all day but were left isolated because no one else could keep up. Matti would be there but was untried, so that would be interesting. He definitely couldn't make things worse! Ahmed and Paul were at about the same skill level, and Paul had no qualms about subbing himself as and when necessary.

He sent out a WhatsApp with his idea for the team and asked if anyone had any problems with it. Tiler and Ahmed, who were working with him, said it was looking good. Bethan, who was covering the signallers' breaks, agreed. Roll on Monday!

Paul turned to go on his break but collided with Andy who had stealthily appeared behind him. 'Bloody hell, Andy. Please stop doing that!' The others looked across, apparently as surprised as Paul to see Andy.

'You're not in today, are you?' Paul asked.

'No. Gav rang me to say this guy had taken the Jet Ski and he had the car; said to meet him in the car park in ten minutes.'

'I think you're fuckin' mental,' Tiler chipped in. 'He'd sell his grandmother if he could make a buck, that one.'

Ahmed was nodding but didn't comment.

'D'you think this is wise, Andy?' offered Paul more reasonably. 'I mean, a Jet Ski for a black BM, and then he sells the BM straight to you. It all sounds a bit, well, suss. What d'you think?'

'Maybe, but I gotta have a car, and I don't have the time to go searching for one. Gav'll cut me a nice deal.'

'The only thing he'll cut is your throat for a quid, the fucking conning bastard,' offered Tiler. 'Make sure you check the brake pipes; he may have cut those too!'

Andy pulled his phone out of his pocket. 'There he is now,' he said, as if Tiler hadn't spoken. 'I'll see you later.'

As he left, Tiler shouted after him, 'Check under the carpets for drugs!'

Paul looked at Tiler and shook his head.

'Absolutely stinks,' said Tiler.

*

When Paul arrived home, Paula was already cooking dinner, in accordance with their 'first home cooks dinner' rule. She had worked the day shift as a senior nurse at the hospital. 'Good day at the office, dear?' she joked.

'Yeah, apart from Tiler and Gav at each other's throats again – could do without that at work. You?'

'Mm. Busy, busy, busy as usual. So many patients, so few beds. I don't know how long we can carry on, I really don't. Michelle didn't come in today because she couldn't afford her childcare fees which then increased the workload for everyone else. This is how it's going now. Evelyn and Stephen are off with stress. Every day there's more like them. I'm just trying to keep all the balls in the air.'

Paul rubbed her arm. 'That's why those who can afford it are going private and those who can't, well, just wait and hope, I suppose.'

'Talking about balls,' Paula said with a laugh, 'how's the footy going?'

'Really enjoying it. Getting the team together, organising everyone and then the game – yeah – it's great.'

'I think you're looking younger already – and thinner,' Paula replied, patting Paul's stomach. 'It's definitely good for you and that horrible odour has gone now you've given up the smoking.'

'Yeah, feeling good – hopefully, I've turned a corner. Anyway, all set for Monday, looks like we'll have a good team out. We're playing the Bankers. And we'll find out who we've got in the second round of the Cup. I can see on the WhatsApp group everyone's excited about that – except Tiler, who can't respond at all on that old phone. But that's Tiler. To be fair, he's out training most days – walking 5K now, apparently.'

'Wow, that's quite an improvement.'

'He told me today his club want him to start walking the Parkrun on a Saturday morning. So, everyone's making an effort, which is exactly what I was hoping for.'

'Fingers crossed for a win on Monday night, then!'

'Yeah, hoping for a win, obviously, but I think we'll be happy if we can just see some gains. Trev's been talking to people this week, and he'll be there, so that will help. Let's see what happens.'

Chapter Eleven

Tiler has the ball; he rolls it to Carl. Carl to Bethan, first-time pass onto Kev's right foot and bang, straight in the back of the net. Then Andy has the ball, quick pass to Bobby Brown, who passes square in front of Kev's left and bang, straight in the back of the net. Kev picks up the ball from Paul in defence, goes left past a defender, right past another, goes left past the last one and bang, straight in the back of the net. The crowd are stamping and shouting, 'Kev, Kev, Kev.' There's banging and mayhem and craziness. 'Kev, Kev, Kev,' is all he can hear as the madness continues.

'Kev, Kev, Kev, you've fallen asleep in your car, you stupid fuckin' prick. Wake up!' Carl was shouting through the windscreen and banging on the roof as Kev slowly came round in the cruellest of ways. As Kev opened the door, Carl said, 'What the fuck were you dreaming about? You were bouncing around in your seat like it was on fire!'

All Kev could manage was a weak 'leave me alone' while he tried to emerge, still groggy, but with the added disappointment it was all a dream.

'Come on, grab your kit. Let's get to it,' said Carl, a bit more sympathetically.

Walking through the car park, they caught up with Paul and Bethan. 'All set?' asked Paul.

'Yeah! Looking forward to a run around tonight,' replied Carl, surprisingly enthusiastic, 'as long as we do our best. Just had to wake this one up from his car.' Kev grimaced. 'Dreamin' about shaggin' a sheep, the way he was jumpin' round in his seat.' Kev grimaced even more.

'You're supposed to refrain before a match, Kev,' said Bethan.

If Kev could have grimaced further, he would have, but he was too embarrassed.

*

Paul led the way from the darkness of a wintry night to the glaring brightness of the pitch lights and the distinctive sounds of indoor football. They had seen Bobby Brown's car outside, so they weren't surprised to see him in his usual spot, with Stella enjoying his attention.

While Paul approached the desk to pay, the rest went to find a table close to the pitches. There was one next to the No-Hopers who had also arrived, but the Ladz chose one a little further away in case someone said something, and it all kicked off. In fact, no other teams sat near the No-Hopers.

As Paul approached with Trev, who had just arrived, he again noticed something odd about the No-Hopers. They sat scattered around their table, not speaking to each other, just staring at their mobiles. They seemed at odds with the general ambience; every other team was either planning their way to victory or in post-mortem mode, trying to figure out where it had all gone wrong.

'Odd bunch,' Paul said under his breath, then his thoughts moved on.

Liz was standing next to Bethan and the others, and, with Paula bringing the boys, they would have extra spectators.

Carl was on the floor in front of Bethan and Liz, demonstrating the different types of press-ups he did in the gym.

'If you're showing off,' said Bethan, 'you know you're wasting your time with us, don't you?' Carl collapsed off a one-armed effort, face-first into a laughing fit.

'My wife, Paula, will be coming tonight, guys,' said Paul.

'Paula?' repeated Carl, looking up from the floor.

'Yeah, Paula.'

Getting up onto his knees, Carl said more slowly, 'Your wife's name is Paula?'

'Yeah, Paula.'

'That's a bit weird. How long did you have to wait for a Paula to come along?' Carl asked.

Paul laughed. 'It just happened.'

'Paul and Paula. I suppose you're never going to forget her name, are you?'

'Could work for you, too,' said Bethan, helping Carl to his feet.

'Oh yeah – Carl and Carla – perfect. I'll hop on Tinder when I get home!'

Matti had just arrived, and Paul could see Andy coming through the main door. He said, 'That's the first time I've seen him approaching. Normally, I turn round and he's standing there.'

'He does that to you too?' asked Matti.

'He does it to everyone – makes out he doesn't know he's doing it,' said Bethan. 'Defo ex-SAS, I reckon.'

'Or just a psycho-killer,' added Kev, starting to come round.

Tiler wasn't far behind Andy – last but not late, for a change. The team was complete, including two subs – which was going to help a lot. Paul called Bobby over to have a pre-kick-off chat. It was good to have Trev there, as he did most of the talking.

After a few minutes, Trev summarised. 'The main things to take from this are, firstly, don't bunch up and, secondly, let the ball do the work like we practised. That way, you won't fatigue, and you're making them run more.'

They all nodded, and Paul took over. 'So, we've got Tiler in goal. We'll start off with Carl and Andy in defence, Beth and me in the middle and Bobby up front, and then mix it up as we go along. Remember, just because you go off doesn't mean it's game over

– you're just having a break. Also, we're here to enjoy ourselves. We want to win, of course, but don't take it too seriously.'

The tannoy boomed, 'FATLADZ TO PITCH NUMBER ONE. BANKERS TO PITCH NUMBER ONE. FATLADZ AND BANKERS TO PITCH NUMBER ONE.'

They stripped off their jackets and tracksuits, revealing their brand-new kit. 'Wow – look at us!' said Andy. 'A vision in blue!'

Bobby laughed. 'Straight from Stamford Bridge.'

Paul grabbed the practice balls, and they made their way to the pitch. He waved to Liz, Paula and the boys, who were shouting for them.

'We've got two minutes. Bobby, take that ball and warm up Tiler in goal, and we'll do some close passing over here.'

'Show time!' growled Tiler.

The two minutes passed quickly, and Paul was soon called to the middle. Only then did he look at the opposition in their pink shirts: two girls, four guys – most youngish, a couple more mature, but all looking good on the ball. One of the girls stood out as her long dark hair, held back from her face by clips, took to the air behind her as she ran. Paul didn't read anything into this display of femininity, as he had seen how sharp, strong and determined the LadyKillers had been the previous week. Also, Bethan was as good as most on a pitch. Male or female was not an issue in this game.

The referee flipped the coin, and the Bankers' captain called tails; it was heads. They shook hands.

'We'll kick off, then,' said Paul, keen to get any advantage they could early in the game.

While they were clearing away the practice balls, Paul noticed they looked like a team now – hopefully, they could put in a decent performance to match. He also noticed the Bisies were standing in the spectators' area.

'Come on, you Ladz!' one of them shouted as Paul passed, and then all the spectators and the subs cheered, a noise which was amplified by the metal roof and concrete walls. Paul watched the whole team look at each other and laugh at this 'first'. Now they felt like a football team.

The ref didn't waste any time as he placed the match ball on the centre spot. Paul and Bobby stood on either side of it. The Bankers lined up quite deep, leaving Paul and Bobby some unexpected space. The whistle blew.

Game on.

Bobby tapped the ball to Paul, and they started to move up the pitch. Bethan came up left and Bobby stayed right, with Carl and Andy walking to the halfway line. But it was never going to be that easy. The Bankers started coming out and putting the three Ladz under pressure with hard physical tackling, which stayed just on the right side of the referee, and it wasn't long before they'd gained possession.

After some midfield tussling, the Ladz found themselves all back, defending Tiler's goal. A shot from the left caught Tiler unsighted, but he managed to get a hand under it to lift it over the backboards, from where it rebounded into the path of their captain who kicked a cannonball. Tiler, though, had anticipated it and was crouching, just legal, at the edge of the area, making himself as big as possible. It hit him hard on the chest, bouncing out to Carl, who turned and kicked it awkwardly up the pitch.

With everyone condensed into the Ladz' half, there were no defenders home to take the ball, as the goalkeepers were confined to their area. Bethan and Bobby reacted first, pursued by two Bankers. It was a foot race between the four, and Bobby won. He swerved to the right, and both defenders unexpectedly followed him, leaving Bethan in space on the left. Bobby got his pass away just before he was tackled heavily to the floor by the girl with the flowing hair, and Bethan was there to side-foot the ball accurately through the flailing left hand of the Bankers' keeper and into the goal at the far post.

The crowd went wild, shouting and cheering. 'Come on, you Ladz! Come on, you Ladz!'

There were high fives all round. They had worked hard to get that goal; things were coming together. Bobby got up, shook himself and half limped, half ran gingerly back to the centre, rubbing the back of his thigh.

'Well done, Beth! Well done, Ladz!' shouted Trev. 'Try and hold on to it 'til half-time. You're doing great!'

And they did just that. They were starting to get battered by the sheer physicality of the game, but they managed to ride the tackles and keep some possession. Although they didn't get another shot on target, they held off the Bankers.

At half-time, Carl and Andy were panting heavily, so Paul took them off; he was also afraid things were going to kick off as the two of them were becoming frustrated with some of the Bankers' tackling.

'I'll come back into defence with Kev,' Paul said. 'Matti, you go with Beth in the middle and … Bobby, you OK?'

'A bit shell-shocked, but I've had worse. It's those two girls; they're mental. It's like being tackled by Roy Keane – twice!'

'You're dead right there,' agreed Bethan.

'Right, you stay up front, Bobby, and we'll see how we do. Trev?'

'So, what we need now is quick passing. You've got to let the ball do the work, and you'll run less. It's easy for me to say, I know – much harder when you're on the pitch – but the more possession we have, the less chance they have of scoring. They're putting in these big tackles, but then they have to get up, turn and start running again. It's not a good way to play, and they're going to tire. When you're thinking it's getting tough, it's going to be tougher for them. And we can't just defend our lead; we have to get up there and keep them honest, so they know we'll punish any mistakes. Also, I notice they've only got one sub, so this is a real chance to achieve our first win. Deep breath, everyone. Come on, you Ladz!'

The referee was already at the centre spot, preparing for the second half, so they all took their positions, and the whistle blew.

The midfield tussling began – back and forth, possession gained, possession lost … Even though Paul had specified where everyone was to play, positions blurred as the game became more fluid. That was how Kev found himself running up the right sideline out of defence, with Bobby calling for the ball in the middle and Paul behind Bobby on the left. Kev neatly lifted the ball over the swinging, outstretched leg of the last defender and ran towards the right corner.

With their captain in close pursuit, Kev stopped the ball dead ten yards short of the goal line, causing their captain to overrun it, unbalanced. As their captain stumbled, he swung out a leg aimlessly and caught Kev above the knee. Kev had a split second to get his pass away as he was falling. It found Bobby in the centre with a flailing, pink-shirted defender coming in hard from behind. Bobby had to act smartly as the dirty tackle came in, so he stepped over the ball which went straight to Paul's feet. Paul managed to control it with his left and let off a solid shot with his right, beating the goalkeeper at the near post.

The cheers broke out again. Two-nil with six minutes to go.

'Keep it tight and keep it moving!' shouted Trev from the spectator area.

Paul was walking back, thrilled. He would have definitely accepted this position if offered to him at the beginning of the night. But as he turned, his heart sank. Kev was standing on one leg, supporting himself on the side wall and rubbing his thigh hard. His wince said it all. Even worse, Bobby was still down after the late tackle from behind.

Paul ran to him and carefully helped him up.

'I went over on my ankle when I got clobbered, the dirty bastards,' Bobby said, as they watched Kev working his way off with the support of Bethan and Matti.

'You two take it easy,' said Paul. 'We'll get Carl and Andy back on; they've had a good break, so no probs.'

As Kev and Bobby were helped into the spectator area, looking dejected, the offending tackler ran over, said sorry to Bobby and tapped him on the back. Bobby didn't reply. 'Bankers? Bloody Wankers, I'd say,' he said to Kev under his breath.

'Definitely,' Kev agreed.

'Back to the way we started, then,' said Paul, 'Except Matti. You stay up to stretch them out, unless it gets really pressured.'

Before the referee restarted the game, he said to the opposing captain, 'If I wasn't playing advantage, both those tackles would've been free kicks.' There was no reply.

So now they had five and a half minutes to hold out.

'Concentrate!' shouted Trev. 'Don't let it go now!'

The game got more physical. Matti couldn't get forward but was working hard in defence, taking the knocks but giving plenty too.

'Come on, Matti!' the supporters shouted from the sidelines.

One of the Bankers, bigger and younger than the rest, took the ball on the halfway line and charged headlong down the left towards Carl, who stood his ground. It was an unstoppable force hitting an immovable object. The massive collision bounced the attacker off an unyielding Carl, and he went sprawling.

'Calm down, sonny,' Carl said, staring at the prone youngster. He pulled the ball back and passed it up to Matti, which led to more midfield to-ing and fro-ing.

The minutes ticked by until, out of nowhere, the ball hit the backboards of the Ladz' goal. The Bankers had scored. While they celebrated, the Ladz were looking at each other, trying to figure out what had gone wrong. One lapse in concentration had let in their opponents.

'Come on; we're still ahead! One minute thirty – don't let it go!' shouted Paul as the game restarted.

The pressure from the Bankers was intense. All the play was in the Ladz' half, and the shots were raining down on Tiler, who was working hard to keep them out.

The Ladz were struggling, and with thirty seconds to go, the inevitable happened. After some quick interpassing, the still-sharp

Bankers had the ball in the back of the net for a second time. There was a groan from the Ladz' spectators and an even bigger one from the players. Paul was pleased that Paula had taken the boys home just before the goal. Just ten seconds remained on the clock. No sooner had the game restarted than the referee was blowing full-time on his whistle.

The Ladz had drawn 2–2 with the Bankers, but they felt like they'd lost. Another late capitulation. The spectators mumbled condolences as the team made their way back to the table, but it was like the Ladz had snatched defeat from the jaws of victory.

'Well done, Ladz!' shouted the captain of the Bisies. 'Great improvement!'

'We should have won,' replied Tiler.

'Hey, don't beat yourselves up. It was a good draw against a hard team to keep down. We lost 4–2 to them, so yours is a good result!'

The whole team sat down while the spectators rallied round to help the wounded.

'Anyone got a bad injury?' asked Paul.

'Probably easier to ask if anyone doesn't have a bad injury,' replied Carl.

'How's the foot, Bobby? Can you walk?'

'Sore, sore, sore,' Bobby lamented. 'What a dirty team they are.'

'Dirty bastards,' Kev groaned in agreement.

'Well, as the Bisies said, don't beat yourselves up,' said Paul. 'It was a good result, and we did well to hold them down at the end. Trev?'

'You were all brilliant. That could have been a thrashing, but you held them right to the end. The fitness is coming. Tiler, you stayed on the whole game, working hard. Every week that passes, we'll get fitter and fitter. Carl and Andy, you played for most of the game and solidly. Beth and Matti, you didn't stop running all game, and Paul, you're always in the right place. With Bobby and Kev both on form tonight, it's the makings of a great team. Got some notes for you all individually, but we can go through those in work. I can definitely say that the next game will be our first win. So don't let your heads drop, as this was a great result.'

The Bankers were walking towards them.

'Here we go,' said Paul, memories of the No-Hopers' barbs still fresh in his mind.

'Hey, cracking game tonight, guys,' their captain said. 'I really thought you had us out there. Only your third game, I believe. Great result for you so soon.'

Tiler couldn't help himself. 'It's cost us a dozen minor injuries and a broken leg to achieve it.'

'Sorry about that,' the Bankers' captain said, his cheeks colouring. 'We spend all day staring at computer screens, grovelling to angry customers shouting at us. So, when they let us out, we get a bit crazy, a bit over the top. Definitely nothing personal.' He held up his hand as the rest of the Bankers mumbled agreement.

'None taken,' said Bobby, massaging his painful ankle propped on a chair.

The Centre manager had walked over while they were speaking. 'We've done the Cup draw for the next round, guys. So, if you're ready, I'll tell you what we've got.'

He looked around for dramatic effect, but it was lost on Tiler, who gruffly shouted, 'Get on with it!'

'OK. FatLadz, you've got P.S.Vehicles. Bankers, you've got the No-Hopers. Enjoy!' He moved to the next table.

'Bugger!' exclaimed the Bankers' captain. 'That's us out, then. I don't know what they're still doing in this competition – really spoils it for everyone else. There's a great bunch of guys and girls here – a terrific community – but that lot are arseholes; no other word for it!' This was echoed by the rest of his team.

'Just get out there and kick the shit out of them like you did to us,' said Tiler.

'Mmm, sounds like a plan,' the captain said, rubbing his chin, 'but catching them first is the problem!' Laughter all round. 'We'll probably see you next week.'

'Definitely,' said Paul. 'Take it easy.'

'Not such a bad bunch,' said Matti, watching them saunter towards the exit.

'Yeah, but we're definitely gonna remember them for a few days, that's for sure,' lamented Kev, still rubbing his thigh.

Bobby Brown had stealthily removed himself and was standing at the counter with Stella. He was pointing to his foot and obviously recounting his heroism which appeared to impress her no end.

'Bloody hell – he's at it again. I'm going over to say something,' said Bethan, shooting up from her chair.

'Leave it, Beth. You can't get involved in other people's relationships,' Carl replied.

'He's right,' added Kev. 'You're the one who'll get the worst of it.'

'Let them sort it out themselves. He is what he is, and they're all adults,' said Andy.

Bethan threw herself back into her chair with a huff.

Tiler shook his head. 'These boys don't give a shit, Beth. They just don't want any hassle. I say, go get 'em! Go on; sort 'em out, Beth!'

Bethan pursed her lips and stayed where she was, to the clear relief of the rest of the team.

Paul quickly changed the subject. 'OK, plan for the next week: Keep your individual training going because we *are* getting there – we *can* do this – we *can* compete with these guys. I'll check the roster to pick the team for next week's Cup match but let me know if you aren't available for any other reason. I'm going to stay and watch P.S.Vehicles – they're on the main pitch at eight thirty if anyone wants to stay – see what we're facing. Anyone else want to say anything?'

Nobody stepped forward.

'Dismissed.'

*

'So, I stayed to watch our opponents in the Cup,' Paul said, squeezing toothpaste onto his brush. 'On a good day, I think we'd stand a chance. Everyone's on board and trying their best, that's for sure.'

Paula threw a face wipe into the bin. 'You all looked great in that new kit. Just can't believe you didn't win after we left. Are you going to tell the boys?'

'Only if they ask. I mean, we didn't lose, did we? Did they enjoy it?'

'Very much so, but they had homework to do, so I brought them home. They want to start a team down there themselves. With their school friends.'

'There's a great atmosphere – it would be good for them. I think they have the kids playing on a Saturday morning.' He waggled his toothbrush. 'There's something going on, though – something not so good.'

'You mean at the football?'

'Yeah. Could become a problem.'

'What?'

'Bobby Brown has taken up with one of the women behind the refreshments counter …'

'He's not doing it again, is he? Honestly. How *old* is he, for heaven's sake?'

'Yeah, up to his tricks. They seem to be getting quite thick together. I saw him leave with her. The boys just about held Bethan back from confronting the woman. She's called Stella. None of us are very happy about it, but Beth seems to be taking it almost personally. Not sure what's going on with her.'

'Well, ask her,' suggested Paula.

'I might if I get the chance. I'll tell her not to take it so much to heart, because no one will be able to stop her next time, that's for sure.'

Chapter Twelve

Paul was standing by Andy's desk, watching the morning rush-hour trains on his screen as they threaded their way through the busy mainline junction. 'How you feeling after last night, Andy?'

'Stiff and sore. Haven't had such a physical workout since the Army. I think we did well, though; some good saves from Tiler kept us in the match.'

Tiler, on the central desk, perked up. 'Trying my best. How's the car going for you?'

'Don't talk to me about that bloody car!'

'I told you he was a fucking conman,' Tiler replied self-righteously. 'He'd sell anything to anyone if it made him a quick buck.'

Paul walked back to his desk, not yet ready for one of Tiler's rants.

'I know, but I needed a car. Anyway, Ahmed's coming down later to have a look at it. Hopefully, it's not expensive; I'm really short at the moment,' Andy said miserably.

'What did Gav say about it?'

'He said it was OK when he sold it to me. He'd driven it himself when he made the exchange.'

'He's a fucking liar, too. What's the problem with it?'

'There's a tapping coming from the engine.'

'That's not too bad.'

'And a metallic sound on the brakes, which are really poor.'

'Well, could be something simple.'

'And—'

'Hold on, I'm finishing at six, y'know—'

'And I have to park it facing downhill. Outside my house. If it doesn't start, I can bump it. I mean, it does start fifty per cent of the time.' Andy gave a self-conscious laugh.

'Fifty per cent!' exclaimed Tiler. 'You gotta have reliable transport in this job. I'll fuckin' tell him when I see him.'

'Leave it, Tiler. It's my problem. Cars – I hate 'em. I'll see what Ahmed's got to say later.'

Daniel was covering breaks and was about to cook them something nice before he left. Dudley arrived to take Matti through the different systems of signalling that have been used to keep trains safe over the years. Dudley had been directly involved with most of them over his long service.

'Make sure you listen to Dudley, young Matti; he's done all this stuff.' But before Dudley could start, Tiler ploughed on.

'Y'see, the problem now is that we've got a flawed system designed by the Tories. These rolling-stock companies own all the rolling stock, and they rent it out to the operating companies. Then *we* charge the OCs to run *their* trains on *our* tracks. These companies are bloodsuckers; multinationals creaming off hundreds of millions of pounds through tax havens which should be coming back to us to improve the railway. Then it's left to the taxpayer, Joe Public, the season-ticket holder, to pay ridiculous prices to cover the shortfall, while we have to run unreliable and overloaded trains. And that's if they run at all.'

'Tiler used to be the union rep,' Dudley said to Matti.

Tiler continued. 'I had to finish because it was making me ill and angry. Another thing that infuriates me – if you look close enough, you'll find some of these Tories making their fortune off this racket; I guarantee it. It's a fucking travesty. Add to that the ridiculous tit-for-tat fining system where we fine the OCs for, for instance, a train failure, and then they fine us for, say, a points failure, and you've got a right old mess.' He was now in his conference speech mode. 'That's why they continue to cut, cut and cut again, and that's why the British public will pay for, but never have, the efficient and reliable railway they deserve.'

A spontaneous round of applause broke out from Dudley, Paul and Andy, and then Matti joined in.

'I'm gonna sit down; I'm getting angry,' said Tiler, tapping his palm on his chest.

'Wouldn't it be better if it was all owned by the government, so all the profits could come back in?' asked Matti.

'I'm voting for *him!*' shouted Dudley, and the rest cheered.

*

Ahmed arrived after lunch. Paul shot Andy an encouraging smile. Poor guy; he didn't deserve it if he was being done over by Gav.

Andy threw the car keys to Ahmed. 'Dreading what you're gonna say, mate.'

The door slammed, and the mood in the room changed instantly.

Gerry boomed, 'What are you doing here, Ahmed? You're not on duty.'

'He's come to look at my car,' said Andy.

'What? This isn't fucking Halfords, y'know! This is a place of work, and you lot should respect it more.' Gerry's phone beeped, and he studied the screen. 'Oh, and I hear your ... team'—Gerry indicated quotation marks for the word—'lost again.'

He was one of those people who could get under your skin with just a few words.

'We didn't lose; it was two all,' Matti said.

'You didn't win, though, did you?' Gerry bounced back right in Matti's face. 'I told you from the start you were knocking your heads against a brick wall trying to organise anything here.'

'... *and* we got half-kicked to death doing it,' Matti persevered.

'Hold on. You scored two goals?'

'Paul scored one, and Beth scored the other.'

'What? Bethan? For fuck's sake! You're having to rely on a girl to score goals for you? I've heard everything now. What a bunch of fucking failures! I'm up at Head Office for the rest of the day, so don't ring me.' He turned on his heel and was gone.

'That was mercifully short,' said Dudley.

'Thank heavens,' agreed Matti. 'I've never disliked anyone before. Now I can't stand to be in the same room as him. Unfortunately, I have to toe the line, as he'll be doing my reports.'

'Hopefully they'll give him his marching orders up there at Head Office,' said Andy. 'We used to call it DCM in the Army – Don't Come Monday!'

Paul chuckled. 'More likely they'll tell him, "You're doing a great job," and give the bugger a pay rise!'

He was figuring out the roster for the following week, trying to see who was available for the Cup match. He was disappointed to see Bethan and Carl would be missing. One or two would always be working, but he had a good pool of players and could fall back on the others who were available.

As it stood, providing no one else was unavailable, he would have Tiler, Andy, Ahmed, Gav, Kev, Bobby Brown, depending on his injury, Matti and himself. But it was only Tuesday, and everyone was still getting over the kicking they'd received from the Bankers. On the WhatsApp group, though, they were thrilled with how the game had gone and that they'd managed such a result in spite of the dirty play.

*

A little later, Matti was on his way home and Daniel was in the kitchen when Ahmed reappeared.

Andy's eyes widened. 'OK, give it to me. Do I need to sit down?'

When Ahmed laughed, Paul saw Andy's shoulders relax. 'I'll give it to you right between the eyes!' Andy's shoulders tensed again. 'There's nothing left of the brake pads, which is the metallic noise you're getting, and they've gone on to warp the discs. The tapping is probably just some adjustment needed in the head, and the battery is way down. It's charging fine, but it's way past its use-by date. I'd need to get new discs and pads and a new battery. If I can get them trade, it'll be about one-fifty if we're lucky; two hundred if not. I think you'll have a half-decent car then, Andy.'

Tiler, on the west-end desk, grimaced. 'He's still a fucking conman.'

'Could have been worse, I suppose,' said Andy. 'When d'you think?'

'I've had a guy cancel a job for this Saturday afternoon – any good?'

'I'm here all day Saturday.'

'Don't worry. I'll come here and do it in the car park; I've got all the kit in my van.'

'Great. Gerry's not around on a Saturday, so you'll have some space down there. Thanks, Ahmed.'

'No probs. See you then.'

Dudley said to Andy, 'We're so lucky to have Ahmed. He saves us an absolute fortune.'

'I know,' replied Andy. 'He's the best. He could make a lot of money if he went out on his own.'

'He asks for some strange things in return, mind you,' Dudley continued. 'Apparently, he asked Carl to get him a chess set 'cause he and his missus play a lot and his kids are learning. Carl had seen him reading Tolkien recently, and he got him a real quality *Lord of the Rings* set; spent about seventy quid.'

'Sounds good. When he serviced Liz's car for Bethan, he asked for a new pack of spanners. Small price to pay, though. I'm crossing my fingers the car isn't too bad.'

Dudley nodded and turned to Paul. 'What's the score for your

Cup match next week? Got a full team?'

'Yeah, looks like Carl and Beth will be working, though, so it'll be a night off for them. Probably best to keep her and Bobby Brown apart for a while, anyway.'

'Don't tell me,' said Dudley. 'Bobby Brown's screwing around again, and Beth doesn't like it.'

'In a nutshell. How did you know?' asked Paul.

'Heard a couple of things through the grapevine. It probably goes back to her father.'

'Her *father?* What's he got to do with it?'

'Just some chat I heard, so not for me to say, really. She'll tell you herself if she wants to, I expect.'

Paul was puzzled, but he didn't press Dudley. The guy was right; it wasn't for him to gossip. 'So, back to the team,' Paul said. 'We should be OK, as we'll have at least two subs. That's important, as this short, sharp running can tire out even the fittest players, and there's a high chance of injury, too. If we can keep a full team on, we're in with a shout. Matti was a revelation last night, so with him and Bobby Brown up front, anything could happen. I'm getting excited just talking about it.'

Dudley nodded. 'There's plenty of enthusiasm for it, that's for sure, and not just amongst the players. It's a topic of conversation even when none of you are around. If you could get that idiot editor on your side, there'd be a lot more on board, I can tell you that for nothing.'

'Well, no one's been in touch today, so we won't be in it. But it *was* one of the things I wanted, you know, to get people interested in us being, well, like a big family again, I suppose. Management have spent so much energy on dividing and ruling over the past decades, it's left little spirit in us. We've lost the camaraderie on the back of email, Teams and now AI. *And*, when you've got morons like this editor guy steering the ship, you just know everyone's going to end up in the sea!'

'Never mind, Paul; Gerry's commanding the rescue boat!'

Dudley replied.

'Yeah,' said Paul, laughing. 'Gerry'll save us!'

There was a lull in the conversation.

'Shit!' Paul grabbed his forehead. 'Shit, shit, shit!'

Andy and Dudley turned to him. 'What's the matter?' they said in unison.

'Gerry's gone up to Head Office today. That's where the newsletter comes from.'

'He wouldn't, would he?' said Dudley.

They all knew he *would*, and he probably *had*! Paul hurried to the computer to see if it had come through. And there was the headline:

A LEAN NIGHT FOR THE FAT LADS!

Paul clicked through to the article:

Oh dear, what can the matter be?

The Fat Lads are stuck in the lower league!

They just cannot cobble together a win, can they? Even a team of bankers, that's 'bankers', not what you thought, proved too big a challenge; they must have been up on their Black Horse!

There was controversy during the game when the Bankers were kicked to high heaven as the Fat Lads tried to get some possession to score their goals.

Come on, Fat Lads, time to shed some 'pounds'. Let's see you 'cheque' yourselves and 'deposit' a few in the back of the net!

Give us a win or rap it in!

Paul's heart sank. 'Some people just suck the fun out of everything. Well, we know whose work that is, for sure. They must have been laughing their heads off producing that pile of crap.'

'It's like you're being trolled,' added Dudley.

'Gerry must have something on this editor guy,' suggested Andy. 'I mean, why would someone be so venomous about something so, well, worthy?'

Paul shook his head slowly. 'I don't know, really I don't. But I *will* find out!'

*

'I'm fucking fuming,' cried Bethan. 'Who the fuck does this arsehole think he is?'

It was Thursday morning, and Paul, Bethan and Carl were on duty. Carl was training Matti.

'As soon as Daniel comes in, I'm getting straight on the phone. Don't try and stop me this time.' The mood she was in, Paul didn't consider interfering. 'He's just printing exactly what Gerry tells him!' she continued. 'And why is Gerry so bitter and negative? I'm so pissed off!'

'Totally unnecessary,' said Carl.

She huffed. 'I've realised that I've met this idiot.'

'You met him?' echoed Carl.

'Yeah. It's Lawrence something, isn't it? I can't remember his surname. While I was training, I had to go on an HR Appreciation Day.'

'Run that by me again,' said Carl.

'Human Resources run these days so we can all go up to see how important they are,' explained Paul.

'You are fuckin' jokin' me,' replied Carl, eyes wide.

'Anyway,' Bethan continued, 'he was one of the speakers. I'll tell you who he looks like – I saw it straightaway. D'you remember that guy who played the Gestapo man in Indiana Jones – the one with the coat hanger?'

'It was, er, Ronald ... Ronald Lacey?' suggested Paul.

'That's him – him, but sweatier!'

'Urgh!' grimaced Carl.

'Anyway, the main thing he was talking about was communication and this bloody all-singing, all-dancing, interactive, multimedia newsletter he'd designed and organised. He really bigged it up, but at the end of the day, it was just a daily staff briefing like we had in prison. I remember him more for how he was at lunch, though. He couldn't look the girls in the eye when making conversation. He'd just be there checking out their tits. Even mine!'

Carl drew a breath to speak, and Paul put his hand up. 'Don't say a word!' he said, and they all laughed.

'Everyone felt uncomfortable around him. With all those pretty young HR girls looking up to him as a senior member of staff, he must have thought all his birthdays had come at once. And it wasn't just the girls; some of the guys said the same. So, that was the talk in the toilets, then one of the girls called him Leering Larry the Lecher. That stuck!'

'Leering Larry the Lecher,' repeated Carl, laughing with the others.

'What happened at the end, Beth?' asked Matti. 'Just in case I have to go on one.'

'I didn't stay 'til the end.'

'You walked out?'

'Well, I couldn't believe it! They gave us a few pieces of Lego and said we should build a small model to take away to our office as a reminder of what we'd learnt during the day. What a load of absolute bollocks! That wasn't what I joined the company for. They operate on a completely different planet, totally alien to normality. I got up and walked out – left them to it – fuck them!'

There was laughter all round.

'So,' said Carl, 'the system is screwed, we have to strike for any kind of decent pay rise, our conditions are being eroded every year, the public are being ripped off left, right and centre, and this bunch are having a day out building fucking Lego. Unbelievable!'

'Nero played while Rome burned,' said Paul. He didn't want to add fuel to Bethan's fire, but he was still angry about the newsletter.

'D'you know what?' said Carl. 'I haven't got a sigh big enough.'

Matti's face was solemn. Paul wondered if he was considering a career change.

As they were all starting to calm down, Daniel arrived. Softly spoken as ever, he asked, 'Who's on first break?'

'Me,' said Bethan gruffly. She explained a few things to Daniel, grabbed her phone and marched to the messroom. She clearly wasn't going to let the grass grow under her feet.

'D'you think someone should go and make sure she doesn't get herself sacked, Paul?' asked Carl.

'She knows the score.' Paul paused. 'I'll give it a couple of minutes then go in and make some tea.'

As Paul approached the door, he heard Bethan's raised voice. On entering, he was surprised to see Gerry. He must have come up in the lift and, judging by the clipboard, he was doing his monthly fire safety checks. It clearly wasn't bothering Bethan.

'... what's really pissed me off is that you came on the phone to me all nicey-nicey, and then you wrote the most negative, condescending load of shit I've ever read. You should be supportive and encouraging, not destroying us, belittling us. So, what I want to know is, firstly, what happened after you spoke to me, and secondly, why are you persecuting us like this? Well?'

Bethan's phone was on loudspeaker and Paul could hear someone trying to speak at the other end but struggling to get their words out, '... deny all those ideas that I'm against y—'

'You spoke to Gerry, didn't you?' Gerry's head twitched to one side, but he didn't turn around. 'You spoke to Gerry, he poured the poison in, and you went with it, you spineless prick. Has Gerry got something on you? Is that it?'

More denials came from the other end, then, 'If you carry on speaking to me like this, young lady, I'm going to terminate this conversation and report y—'

'We've met, you know.'

'Have we? When? I'm sure I'd remember.'

'It was at the HR Day. You'd been speaking. You wouldn't remember me; my tits are too small.'

Paul put a hand to his face. What would she say next? Gerry was staring at the wall.

'I beg y—'

'You spent the whole day staring down all the girls' tops – so

much so that they christened you 'Leering Larry the Lecher'! Did you know that? You even made some of the guys feel awkward. I've got five girls who are prepared to say how uncomfortable you made them feel that day, and they want to take it to Disciplinary.'
Bethan mouthed 'I haven't!' to Paul, shaking her head.

'That's a damn li—'

'We both know it's the truth, and I've got the witnesses to take it all the way. No one will support you, and your fun will be over, as will your career.'

'You can't speak to me like—'

'All I want you to do is publish decent and honest match reports with no spin and no consultation with anyone, particularly the poisonous Gerry Spratt'—she stared at the back of Gerry's head—'and I might be able to talk them out of it.'

The door slammed as Gerry left.

'This is coercion, blackmail of the worst kind'—Paul was thinking that Bethan's time in the prison wasn't wasted—'I absolutely refute all your allegations.' Lawrence was talking faster now. 'They have no base in truth whatsoever. I have a lot more influence here than you may think, young lady. However,' he said more slowly, 'I will go along with what you say.' He paused, seeming to gather his thoughts. 'What shall we call it? A goodwill gesture.'

'Call it what you like. After each match, I'll send you the details, and you put it together in a nice, positive report. That's all I want. And remember, if you're thinking of screwing us over,' Bethan paused, 'just think about Leering Larry the Lecher.'

'I'm sure we'll get along fine. What was your name again, young lady?'

'Bethan – with a capital 'B' – as in *Bitch*!'

She ended the call and shivered. 'Yuck!'

'Remind me never to fall out with you, Beth,' said Paul, placing a mug of tea in front of her.

Chapter Thirteen

As soon as Paul walked into the Football Centre, he sensed a different atmosphere. Initially, he could not put his finger on why it felt so different. Then he realised there was a tension about the place and, on thinking about it, he felt tense too.

The Ladz had joined the League with only a few games to play and were never going to achieve much there, so it would be great to do something in the Cup. But it was amazing they were playing football at all! While he was paying at the desk, he mentioned the change in atmosphere to the Centre manager.

'Cup nights are always a bit different,' he replied. 'It's the pressure. Everyone wants to do well, because on the night of the final, we always push the boat out for the last game of the season. Everyone wants to be playing in it.'

Paul crossed the rest area and found a table. Bobby Brown, not surprisingly, was the first to arrive. 'How's the foot, Bobby? Did you get to the physio?'

'Yeah. I don't know if it'll go a full match; I may have to come off. I'll see how the game goes. Hopefully, it won't be as dirty as last week.'

'God, no! We'd be dropping like flies.' Paul looked across and could see Andy approaching with Gav; some of the others were not far behind.

'Here comes Andy and—' He turned to speak to Bobby, but

he'd already gone. Paul didn't need to look to know where.

'I was just saying to Gav,' Andy said as they approached, 'I was so glad Gerry didn't come up today. Saturday was bad enough. I couldn't have restrained myself again today. I mean, when was the last time Gerry came into the office on a Saturday?'

'Gerry in the office on a Saturday? What happened? Was it that bad?' asked Kev.

'Oh yeah, and worse. He gave poor Ahmed a right bollocking. I don't know what's the matter with the guy. Why can't he just live and let live? Gerry was really annoyed that Ahmed had completely dismantled everything right in front of his office window where he parks. He really took exception to that. By the time he came up, he was red in the face and ranting like an idiot. We couldn't understand a word.'

'Even worse than usual, then,' said Kev.

'Yeah, something about wasters and layabouts and lots of "D'you know whats". He was on about a meeting he was having.'

'On a Saturday?'

'I know. When did Gerry last have a meeting on a Saturday? The whole thing was bizarre.'

'So, who came to this "meeting"?'

'We didn't see,' replied Andy. 'From under the car, Ahmed only saw his legs, but he said this guy turned up at about two thirty and left about forty-five minutes later when Ahmed was under the bonnet. Then Gerry left not long after, to our relief. Someone's gonna flip soon if he doesn't lighten up. Couldn't even leave it as he went. Had another go at Ahmed: "Get this cleared up by Monday before I get in, otherwise I'll wipe the fucking oil up with *you*!"'

'What a fucking prick,' said Kev.

'What about the car?' asked Gav.

'Ahmed did the brakes, the tapping noise and the battery for two hundred and twenty. He's so good at that stuff. He could make a fortune if he set up on his own. Said he's afraid of not getting the business and having to come back, cap in hand. Gerry really upset him, though. Ahmed was completely stressed out when he came up after finishing. We had to sit him down and make him a brew.'

'And the car?' Gav asked.

'Great job – real tidy – no mess.'

'What about the labour cost?' asked Kev.

'Said he'd get back to me on that, so no idea what he'll ask me to get. You know what he's like.'

'Yeah. So, how's the car going now?' Gav said, persevering.

'Like a dream,' said Andy.

'Wait 'til I see that fucking Tiler. I'll stick his "conman" right up his arse!'

Kev laughed. 'You're in luck. Here he comes with Ahmed.'

Andy nodded at Ahmed. 'I was just telling them about Saturday.'

'Ah, man, that guy, he's not stable. There was no need for any of it. I mean, when did we last see Gerry on a Saturday?'

'Yeah,' said Andy, 'and that clandestine meeting. Strange.'

'I've never seen anyone rant like that,' Ahmed added. 'I thought he was gonna have a stroke. And then he had a go at me as he was leaving. I think he's on the edge, y'know?'

'Well, if he stays there, one of us'll be pushing him over it, that's for sure!'

Tiler barked across the table, 'All your fucking fault, Gavin!'

'M-my fault?' Gav spluttered.

'If you hadn't sold Andy such a shit car, he wouldn't have needed Ahmed, and none of this would have happened.'

'I sold that car in good faith with no guarantees.'

'I still say you're a fucking conm—'

'That's enough, boys,' Trev said, rolling his eyes. 'It's football tonight; let's get to it.'

'Yeah, come on, guys,' said Paul. Things could flare up between Gav and Tiler at the drop of a hat *and* with little reason.

'And it's Gav, not Gavin,' Gav muttered, clearly still wanting the last word.

'OK, we're playing P.S.Vehicles,' said Paul. 'I watched them last week. They haven't got a regular goalie – they just swap occasionally – so that's something in our favour. What they have got, though, is six good outfield players who can hold on to the ball for long periods, nearly always ending with a shot at goal, so be alert for that. Tiler, you're doing great in goal, so you hold on to the gloves. Me and Andy, we'll stay back. OK, Andy?'

'I know my place.'

'Ahmed and Gav, you go midfield, and Matti, you go up front to start. Bobby – for God's sake. Call him over, Ahmed.'

Bobby arrived at the table as if he had only just remembered there was a match on.

'Right, Bobby, you start on the bench, as we might need you to get us out of trouble in the second half – I don't want to take a chance on that injury. But we'll see how it goes.' As an afterthought, Paul added, 'Don't wander off in case we need you urgently. Kev, you start on the bench, but I don't think you'll be there long. There's a lot of running to be done tonight. Oh, hi, Liz. Didn't expect to see you here tonight with Bethan not playing.'

'Hi, everyone. I really enjoyed it last week, and Beth wants me to write some details for her to do a report.'

'You'd better make sure it's spot on after the way she tore into that guy last week!' Paul laughed. 'Trev?'

'Right,' Trev began. 'Everyone's doing great. We're starting to function as a team. As I said last week, when we've got possession, let the ball do the work. You're still not doing it enough, but when you do get it right, it's keeping the running down to the bare minimum. When they've got possession, come back basketball style to block them out with numbers. We can review it at half-time. Oh, and Gav and Tiler, try and remember we're all playing for the same team. After these matches tonight, it's the semi-finals. We can do this. Good luck, everyone.'

'FATLADZ TO PITCH NUMBER TWO. P.S.VEHICLES TO PITCH NUMBER TWO. FATLADZ AND P.S.VEHICLES TO

PITCH NUMBER TWO.'

They stripped down, looking the biz in their clean blue kit, and made their way to the pitch.

'Show time!' announced Tiler as they walked onto the pitch.

'Arsehole,' said Gav under his breath.

*

As soon as Paul threw out the practice balls, Kev grabbed one and started warming up Tiler in goal. The others practised sharp passing under Trev's direction. Although the spectator area was small, Paul noticed most of the Bankers and some of the Bisies had squeezed in.

'Come on, you Ladz!' someone yelled.

'We're getting a bit of a fan club,' shouted Matti, and they all acknowledged it with a 'Yay!' and thumbs-up.

This was followed by a quieter cry of: 'Come on, Sebastian!'

There were a few blank looks, then Matti said sheepishly, 'That's my mum.'

'Yeah, but who's Sebastian?' said Tiler with a grin.

Paul won the toss, and the warm-up was over. Bobby and Kev found a place next to Liz, who had her Canon ready to snap some pictures and write notes for Bethan. Trev looked on edge, hoping for the best.

It was game on. Only when the ref blew his whistle did Paul realise just how much this meant to him. Matti kicked off, and immediately they were in the thick of it. Those boys were fast and constantly threatening the Ladz' goal. Every attack ended with a shot on target, always accurate and powerful. But Tiler was really up for it, at times using his bulk and at others diving this way and that. Each time the Ladz tried to advance, it fizzled out; they struggled to get over the halfway line before losing possession, then the cycle began again.

Trev was shouting from the sideline, 'Get your passing going!

Let the ball do the work!' but in the intensity of the fray, nobody picked up on it.

P.S.V. had no subs; they just rotated as goalkeeper. During one of their swaps, Paul took the opportunity to bring on Kev so Andy could have a break, as he was being run ragged by these speedsters.

'You go mid; Ahmed, you come back,' he called as Kev came on. Paul was hoping the extra speed from defence might create something. Also, it kept Tiler and Gav apart.

The rest of the first half was much of the same, except that some of the Ladz' attacks, with the extra speed from Kev, made it well into the P.S.V. area. Unfortunately, even with his mother cheering him on, Matti couldn't finish them off.

Both teams received a solid round of applause as the half-time whistle went. They changed ends and picked up their water bottles. Trev rushed on to make the most of the short time between halves.

'Why aren't any of you listening to me? You've got to get those passes going. I can see from the sideline – they've got no strategy, no plan. They're bunching. You could beat three of their guys with one good pass, then it's just one shot to score. Stop running and start thinking. It's like chess out there. Faster, but basically the same.'

'Everyone got that?' said Paul. There were nods all round as the Ladz took on some much-needed water. 'You all set, Bobby, or d'you want to sit it out for this week? How's the Achilles feeling?'

'I think I'll be OK, boss,' he replied. 'Maybe six to eight minutes.'

'Get some gentle stretches done, and I'll get you on in a couple of minutes.' Paul was hoping not to use Bobby for fear of aggravating his injury. He would see how the first two minutes went.

Trev's wise words started to make sense almost immediately. After P.S.V. kicked off and moved close to the Ladz' goal, Kev was quick and intercepted a short pass. He spotted Matti running up the left wing and hit a perfectly weighted pass just in front of him. With only a flummoxed goalkeeper to beat, Matti fired left and high. In a normal-sized goal, he would have scored, but he hit the top of the post, and the ball rebounded to the sideline. There was a groan from players and spectators, as Matti put his head in his hands. They all knew it was a chance sorely missed.

'Sorry, guys,' Matti drawled as he ran back, mouth downturned.

'Never mind. Put it behind you, and get on with the game,' Trev shouted from the sideline.

Gav was tiring from covering everything at the back with Ahmed and Paul, so, as chances were rare and had to be taken, Paul took the gamble of bringing on Bobby for Gav. He knew it was risky bringing on another attacker in favour of a solid defender, but they needed a goal, and they needed it urgently.

The Ladz started to get their passing together and out-manoeuvre P.S.V. The play moved from the Ladz' goal area, which had seen most of the action, to inside the P.S.V. half. Then some neat inter-passing, which had started from Tiler and gone through the whole team, found Bobby unmarked outside the righthand post, and an easy tap in was his for the taking. It was 1–0!

The spectators cheered and shouted, and the players jumped for joy. All their hard work in defence had paid off.

Almost from the restart, there was confusion amongst the P.S.V. players, which led to Paul intercepting a pass just inside the Ladz' half. From the corner of his eye, he saw Ahmed running up the left sideline and placed his pass perfectly. Three defenders followed the ball, and by stretching, Ahmed diverted it first touch towards Bobby who had parked himself just outside the area on the right. It was another easy tap in for Bobby. 2–0.

More cheers followed, and for the first time, Paul became optimistic. They really had a chance. He was surprised how quickly P.S.V.'s attitude had changed. Even with the barking of their captain, their body language was that of a beaten team. Even though they were all still physically capable, mentally they'd already lost. This became evident from a sloppy kick-off when Kev slid in to stop a tired through pass from the left back. Kev took control of it and, spotting Bobby on the left, ran diagonally towards the right corner flag. With the keeper filling his space, he hit it sharp and flat along the floor to Bobby. So accurate was the pass, that Bobby just had to let it hit his outstretched foot, and then the speed of the ball rebounded it into the empty net. 3–0.

They were three of the easiest goals anybody could score with no exertion whatsoever. There was just over three minutes left. Paul decided that, to save any recurrence, he would remove Bobby from the fray. To have him score the three goals with such little effort was a bonus, for sure. Bobby got an ovation walking off the pitch from players and spectators alike; his seven minutes had proved invaluable to the team. Paul called Gav back on and, as he was completely spent himself, he called Andy back on to take charge in defence.

'Matti, you go back up front. Stay alert!' he shouted. 'Don't let it go now!'

Paul needn't have worried. Once again, P.S.V. were sloppy on kick-off and didn't get another shot on target. Andy had recovered from his first-half efforts, and he and Ahmed conducted a solid defence in front of Tiler, whose hands were becoming safer each game. Gav and Kev were easily holding the midfield, and Matti was stretching P.S.V. at the front.

When the referee blew the final whistle, P.S.V. were well beaten. There were handshakes all round as, unlike the Ladz' previous game, there had been no malice in the match. However, P.S.V. looked despondent. Although they'd performed well enough, they'd been well and truly ground down.

'Liz, did you get all that?' Paul asked.

'Yeah!' She laughed. 'But whether Beth will believe it is another question!'

There was a bounce in the Ladz' stride as they headed back to their table with the spectators from the other teams, eagerly dissecting the match. The gist of the chatter was their amazing turnaround after such an unpromising beginning in the League. Paul and Trev were deep in conversation too, thrilled with the night's outcome.

When the spectators had left, Trev tapped a metal water bottle to get everyone's attention. 'Well done tonight,' he started. 'A great game! You all did your bit to wear them down because they were a good side tonight. And Bobby'—incredibly, he was still with them—'fantastic goals.'

'The easiest I've ever scored, boss. Just as well in the circumstances.'

'They may have been easy, but *I* could see that you threw your marker and got yourself into the right place at the right time; that's what made them good goals. And that's not mentioning the passing that led to the goals. Everyone did well. Really pleased. Paul?'

'Yeah, absolutely brilliant tonight, guys. We can build on this next week. I'll check the roster but let me know if you can't play for whatever reason. Beth'll write a report from Liz's notes, so, after his chat with Beth, hopefully that idiot in HQ will publish something approaching the truth this week. Liz, you got some pictures?'

'Yeah, should be some good ones. And I've texted Beth the score, but she thinks I'm winding her up!'

They all laughed.

'Well done tonight, FatLadz.' P.S.V. were walking towards the door. 'Good game, Ladz,' one of them shouted. 'You've got to win the Cup now! We'll see you in the League sometime.'

'Yeah, thanks,' the Ladz chipped in ... except Bobby, who had disappeared.

'Anyone want to say anything?' Paul asked.

Not a peep came from anyone, no doubt all tired and ready to leave.

'Then, dismissed,' said Paul.

As Matti was talking to Gav, his mother approached Paul and Trev.

'I really appreciate what you're doing for Sebastian,' she said.

'Sorry,' replied Paul. 'What do you mean?'

'Before he started with you in the signalling centre, he spent most of his time in his room, playing video games and watching Netflix. Most of his school and Uni friends were either doing the same or had been lucky enough to get a job after they graduated. But since he took this job on, it's transformed him. He loves the work and learning new things, although he did mention the manager is a bit of a handful.'

Paul laughed. 'He's not wrong there.'

She smiled. 'He's also realised he enjoys being part of a team and no longer wants to be alone all the time. Tells me all the stuff that goes on – lots of funny stuff that happens. Then this football is the icing on the cake. He really loves it, really enjoys – I don't know – being part of something. He especially talks about you two managers.'

'Well, "managers" might be pushing it a bit!' Trev laughed.

'He really looks forward to this, and he's started running again, which was also one of his hobbies that had gone by the wayside.'

'Wow,' said Trev, 'that's great news. I didn't realise.'

'He's a great kid. There's a career there if he wants it,' added Paul.

'I just wanted to say thank you. I'll be giving him plenty of encouragement, so hopefully he's got through that solitary phase now. Thank you.' She turned and left with Matti, both chatting about the game.

Trev and Paul looked at each other. 'Wow,' Trev said. 'Great to hear that. He's a good one.'

Paul couldn't help feeling buoyed up by the conversation. He went home with a spring in his step, looking forward to the next game with anticipation.

Chapter Fourteen

The following days and nights were busy in the ROC. Heavy rain and high winds had swept in from the west, causing landslips, fallen trees and flooding, which meant a massive amount of engineering work and problems with the track. As if that wasn't enough, lightning had struck out the electronics, creating another hazard. The winds had brought down power lines and overhead cables, leaving trains trapped, still full of passengers, and freight unable to get to its destination. Other trains were delayed or cancelled, and some were simply stuck. Safety was paramount.

For the signallers, there was no time for chat or banter as concentration levels needed to be high. The phones were constantly ringing, and endless conversations took place to ensure the tracks were safe before any train was allowed to move. Alarms frequently sounded in a cacophony of distorted noise, each representing a new problem.

It was at these times they needed to be calm under pressure and support each other. There were calls from the engineers trying to block the lines to get work done and restore services. On the other hand, Rail Control were attempting to get things moving as soon as possible on a safety-versus-performance tightrope.

These were the tough days; even Gerry's visit had been thankfully brief so as not to distract them. The football was very definitely on the back burner for a couple of days. As the climate was changing, these problems were becoming more of an issue; they could occur at any time of the year, no longer confined to autumn and winter. After shifts like these, the signallers went home completely drained, heads pounding.

On the upside, Bethan had used Liz's notes and sent her report to Lawrence. She'd told Paul she'd received a sickly, overly nice reply to say he'd include it. On Friday morning with things calmed down, Kev asked Paul if anyone had checked out the newsletter.

'No,' he replied, 'the intranet's been down and only just came back on. Have a look.'

'OK. Let me see now. Oh, we've made top headline, Paul.'

'Great. Things are looking up!'

Kev clicked on the headline.

COULD IT BE A CUP RUN FOR THE FATLADZ!?

Yes! The FatLadz! have finally arrived with a great win in the Central League Cup. They ground down the opposition, P.S.Vehicles, to take a 3–0 win and now move into the semi-final to be played in two weeks' time. Three great goals from the injured Bobby Brown were the difference between the sides, but he was well supported by the rest of the team. See pix below.

With Tiler steadying the ship in goal and Captain Paul at the helm, it's looking good, as long as they aren't scuppered by injuries. Admiral Trev is doing an amazing job of conducting strategy from the sidelines.

Also worthy of a mention: Matti and Bobby, brilliant at the front and well backed up by Kev and Lav. Strong defence from Andy and Ahmed held P.S.V. far enough out not to concede any goals. So, it's onward and upward for The FatLadz! as they build towards great things!

Next match:

Central League:

The FatLadz! v. The DrunkSkunks

The Football Centre, The Rec, Monday at 7.30 p.m.

All supporters welcome but come early for a place!!

'Who the fuck is *Lav*?' laughed Kev.

'What's that?' asked Paul.

'This report in the newsletter. It says, "Matti and Bobby, brilliant at the front and well backed up by Kev and *Lav*."'

'Kev and Lav?' Paul walked over. 'Let's see.' He couldn't help but laugh when he saw it. 'Kev and Lav – oh God!'

'I wonder whose mistake it is: Bethan or creepy editor guy? Either way, Tiler's gonna rip the shit out of Gav ... or is it Lav?'

Daniel and Matti couldn't contain their curiosity any longer. They came over and were soon in fits of laughter.

'That's hilarious,' Matti said between guffaws. 'We'll soon find out who messed up because Beth's covering breaks. And I think Gav and Tiler are in tonight.'

'Great,' said Kev. 'Are you cooking for us today, Daniel?'

'Yeah, I'll knock something together. Everybody in?'

'Oh yes,' said Kev. 'Wouldn't miss one of your brekkies, that's for sure!'

They all agreed and slowly returned to their now quiet workstations.

'By the way,' added Daniel nonchalantly. 'My wife entered me into *MasterChef*, and I've got through to the preliminary stages.'

'What?' they all replied in unison.

'Bloody hell, Daniel!' said Kev. 'Were you going to tell us, or what?'

'Well, yes, of course. Just a bit worried in case Emily has an attack while I'm away.'

'That's understandable,' said Paul, 'but you've got to take the opportunity. We've been saying for ages that you're a cut above – wasted talent here.'

'Hundred per cent,' added Kev, 'you can't let that opportunity pass, Daniel. Go for it!'

'Thanks. We'll see how it goes, anyway.'

Bethan appeared from around the screens. 'See how what goes?'

'It's Daniel,' replied Andy. 'He's only got on to *MasterChef*!'

'The preliminaries, Beth,' added Daniel.

'That's amazing,' she enthused. 'You'll be brilliant.'

'I'm a bit nervous, but I'll do my best. Got a few more stages to go through yet.'

'So – a special brekky this morning?' asked Kev.

'I'm a bit nervous, but I'll do my best!' Daniel repeated, laughing. After handing over to Bethan, he left for the shops.

'He'll be brilliant on that; he's sharp as a knife on food,' she said.

'Hey, Beth, seen the newsletter?' asked Kev.

'No, but I hope Leering Larry's printed it exactly as I wrote it.'

'Well, I don't know. You'd better have a look at it.'

She gritted her teeth. 'What's he done?'

'I've printed out a copy. It's on top of the computer,' Kev replied, walking away from the danger area.

She picked up the sheets of paper and read through the article. '*Lav?* Fucking *Lav?* I'll give him fucking Lav. Why couldn't he just copy and paste it without pissing about with it. Bastard!'

The boys were becoming uneasy; no one liked to be in the room when Bethan was stirring.

'I'll be fucking ringing him later. He knew what he was doing. Gav is going to go spare, and Tiler's going to— bollocks!'

'Beth,' said Kev from the other side of the room, a slight quiver in his voice. 'It was definitely him, was it?'

'Whaat? You're not suggesting …'

'Have you checked your draft?' said Paul, helping Kev, who was fading.

'I sent it off my phone,' she said. 'Hold on – I'll show you.'

She began to scroll through her emails then paused to read one. Her face fell.

'Oh, shit,' she simply said. 'Fuck, fuck bollocks, fuck bollocks shit.'

'He did just copy and paste it then, did he, Beth?'

'He did just copy and paste it … yeah,' she muttered distractedly. 'Bastard.' Then a long, thoughtful pause. 'Oh well, what's done is done. Just hope the fallout isn't too bad. Bollocks!'

*

The evening sun was descending behind the huge green gasometer at the far end of the industrial estate as the familiar odours of the tyre factory floated through the window.

'What a fuckin' stench – every bastard night. It's nauseating. They must make their tyres with fuckin' cabbage and rotten eggs mixed with diesel,' said Tiler to Dudley and Gav. 'That's disgusting. I dread to think what they're kicking out from there. Bloody Chinese!'

'I don't think it's Chinese; I think it's American,' said Dudley who was trying to read his book.

'Yeah, that's what I meant – bloody Yanks!'

The operating floor was a much more pleasant place to be now that all the faults and failures had been cleared after the storms of the two previous night shifts. Tiler's workstation was particularly quiet. But the devil makes work for idle hands and soon a bored Tiler was out to irritate his colleagues.

Only an hour into the shift, he was rolling up scrap paper and trying to throw it ten feet into the bin, hoping to get a reaction from Gav and Dudley to his cheers when successful and swearing when not. Two hours into the shift, he'd already eaten all the food he had brought for the night. Three hours into the shift, he wandered over to the computer where the National Newsletter lay in a tray.

'Look at this,' he said, picking it up and flicking through. 'Beth must have done the match report.' Neither of his colleagues answered. 'Oh – I've got a mention. Well done, me,' he quipped.

Gav turned slightly.

'Oh, fuck! Oh, fuck!' Tiler said. 'Who's this new player we've got?'

'Who? What are you talking about?' Too late – Gav had bitten.

'Lav! Who's this fucking Lav?'

'What? Let me see.'

Tiler made it his duty to read it aloud. 'Also worthy of a mention: Matti and Bobby, brilliant at the front and well backed up by Kev and Lav.'

'What? What the hell has she—?'

'Lav, fuckin' Lav. I think it's brilliant.' Tiler was beside himself with glee. 'There you are, I said you were a fuckin' shithouse, didn't I? This proves it!'

'I'll get it sorted tomorrow,' said Gav indignantly, but Tiler wouldn't let it go.

'Yeah, get it out of your cistern!'

'Just fuck off, Tiler. Fuck off, you fucking prick!'

'Let's calm down, shall we, or someone's going to screw up!' Dudley shouted, slamming his book shut on the desk.

Tiler danced back to his workstation. He couldn't believe his luck. He knew Gav was annoyed beyond words, not because of the misprint, but because it had given Tiler his ammunition for the night. As he walked past, laughing loudly and cruelly, he saw Dudley drop his head into his hands.

*

It was Saturday before Paul could sit down with the roster to sort the team for Monday. It was looking good, with only Andy and Ahmed working. It was the best time of year to plan things as holidays hadn't started, so it was only those working who missed out. Paul published the team on the group: Tiler, Paul, Carl, Kev, Gav, Beth, Matti and Bobby Brown. Lots of 'thumbs-ups' came back, so he knew it was a goer.

'What d'you think about the article, Paul?' asked Carl.

'It was a good report until that fatal mistake!'

'I know. Gav was fuming.'

Paul shook his head. 'Must have made for an interesting shift with Tiler on too.'

'Yeah,' replied Carl. 'I saw Dudley before he went home. He said Tiler was on it all night. Really pissed Gav off and drove Dudley round the bend; he looked totally drained. Tiler's too much sometimes.'

'Yeah. I'm sure it'll all be forgotten by Monday evening, though,' said Paul hopefully.

'Oh yeah – I'm sure …'

Chapter Fifteen

'**B**een to the lav, Gav?' were Tiler's first words on arriving for the match. 'You're looking flushed!'

'I had enough of you the other night; just fuck off!' Gav replied, giving Bethan a reproachful stare.

'Sorry, Gav. It was my fault,' she said.

'Don't apologise, Beth. I think it's bloody brilliant!' shouted Tiler.

'Leave it now, boys, and keep the language down; the place is starting to fill up,' said Paul. 'Let's think football. Let's think DrunkSkunks.'

They sat at their usual table. Liz had arrived, and Paula was also coming with the boys. Unusually, Matti hadn't arrived; they figured he was on his way with his mum. Bobby Brown had arrived with Stella, and he was still talking to her by the drinks machine. He had to be physically dragged away by Carl for the team talk.

'Come on, Bobby Brown. Your missus has chucked you out once, hasn't she?' cajoled Tiler.

'That was a misunderstanding,' Bobby replied indignantly, straightening his shirt.

'Remind me. What was Miss Understanding's name again?'

'Somebody saw me kissing my cousin.'

'Kissing your cousin!' Tiler spluttered. 'That'll get you a prison sentence, mate!'

'It's not illegal.'

'You checked, did you?'

'For God's sake, you two!' barked Paul.

'How's the injury, Bobby?' asked Trev, trying to move on.

'Good,' he replied. 'I don't think it's anything to worry about as I've had plenty of treatment on it.'

'I bet you have, you dirty fu—'

'Give it a break, Tiler,' Paul shouted, exasperated. He didn't want any more hassle; Bobby was valuable to the team. 'Trev?'

'It's the last cycle of League matches tonight,' he began, 'and we've got the DrunkSkunks. We don't know anything about them, except they're mid-table and we were supposed to play them in the Cup, but they couldn't get a team together. We've now found what works for us, so let's stick to it and let them figure us out. Even with a change of personnel this week, we're still strong, so concentrate on sticking to your task, and keep running. Paul?'

'It's Tiler in goal, me and you at the back, Carl. Then Beth and Matti in the middle and Bobby up front. Gav and Kev are on the bench, but not for long, I think. We've got a strong side tonight and, all right, we're not going to achieve anything in the League, but we can use this as a springboard for our next Cup match.'

After Paul finished, he noticed Trev looking wistfully out at the pitch. 'You're still missing it after all these years, Trev.'

'It'll never go away. This is a double-edged sword, for sure. But – you know what I always say.'

'Fuck 'em. Fuck 'em all?' Paul asked.

Trev nodded slowly. 'Exactly that.'

'Matti's late,' said Kev. 'Not like him.'

'No,' said a still-sheepish Bethan. 'His timekeeping is normally bang on.'

'He got caught up in that incident today. That might have something to do with it,' said Gav.

'What was that?' asked Paul.

'Daniel had a fatality on his patch – a suicide, the police reckon, and Matti was out with one of the mobile managers being shown the area when the call came in.'

'Oh, no,' said Bethan. 'Please don't tell me they sent Matti to a fatality.'

'Control didn't want to waste time dropping him off, so he ended up going with the manager.'

'Christ,' said Carl. 'No wonder he's not here. He's only a kid, for God's sake!'

'Poor Matti,' said Liz.

'They were trying to get Gerry for ages. The controller tried, Daniel tried loads of times, and even I was texting him; he just wasn't picking up, so someone had to make a decision. In the end, they told him to go.'

There was a spontaneous silence. They'd all been involved with fatalities on the line, whether as a signaller or attending the scene.

Paul took a deep breath. 'Well, there's nothing we can do now, so let's just get out and win this game. We're down to one sub, so it's going to be a busy night. Kev, you start with Beth in the middle, but Gav, be ready to come on at any time; there's no telling when someone's going to hit the red line.'

'FATLADZ TO PITCH NUMBER TWO. DRUNKSKUNKS TO PITCH NUMBER TWO. FATLADZ AND DRUNKSKUNKS TO PITCH NUMBER TWO.'

'Bloody hell, they're gonna blow someone's head off with that freakin' tannoy one day!' shouted Carl.

'Let's get in there,' declared Paul, removing his tracksuit.

'Show time!' said Tiler.

'Fuck you,' said Gav.

As they walked through the gate and onto the pitch, Paul noticed the small spectator area was almost full. 'Come on, you Ladz!' someone shouted, which was met with a 'Yay!' by the rest of the group. Paul recognised some of the players from their previous opponents. They were recruiting quite a following! Also,

Paula had arrived with the boys and found a space at the front so they could see.

The ref blew his whistle. 'Two minutes,' he shouted as Trev threw out the practice balls. Kev took one down to the goal with Tiler, while the others practised their fast passing. 'Remember, you're one short, so you *have* to let the ball do the work for you,' Trev reminded them.

'OK, boss, no probs,' replied Carl.

With only a few seconds of the warm-up left, Paul turned to Trev. 'At least we've still got one substitute,' he said. As the words left his mouth, he saw Kev chase a bouncing ball before inexplicably trying an impossible overhead kick, which left him writhing on the floor and grasping the back of his leg in agony.

'D'you wanna review that?' Trev replied.

Paul looked back. 'Bugger,' he said, and they walked over to where Kev was laying on the ground, clutching below his right buttock and moaning.

Tiler was leaning over, consoling him. 'You fucking idiot. What the fuck were you thinking of? You've only gone an' fucked up the whole game. You really are a fucking clown!'

Carl helped Kev up, but he was unable to put any weight on his injured leg. The referee had seen what had happened and allowed Paul an extra minute to sort things out. 'One minute, then I'm blowing the whistle.' Typical super-strict ref.

'Now we're screwed,' said Gav. No one disagreed.

Tiler wasn't finished. 'Clown Kev strikes again. What a fucking prick!'

Trev and Carl helped Kev, who was now pale and holding his mouth shut as if about to vomit, over to the small spectator area, where they made room for him to sit down as best he could.

'Our busy night just got a whole lot busier,' announced Paul. 'Gav, you go with Beth in the middle, and for all of us it's going to be run, run, run – and when you think you can't run any further, run some more! I'd really like to do well tonight to take it into next week's Cup match, so come on! We can do this!'

'Try and play up the pitch a bit to force them to find a way through,' suggested Trev. 'That way, you'll still be able to threaten their goal.'

Bethan took the kick-off. She passed it to Bobby, Bobby to Gav, and they were off. The opposition were young, fit and sharp, but the Ladz were catching on to Trev's idea of making the ball work for them. It wasn't long before Bobby engineered a space for himself to the right of the keeper, and from a perfect long pass from Carl through the middle, Bobby scored his first goal. From then, it became an open game, and the 4–4 scoreline at half-time reflected the way both teams were playing. The spectators were loving all the goals and, with more people arriving, the small enclosure was starting to resemble the Kop at Anfield.

'Well done, Ladz,' said Trev as they walked down to their goal, all desperately in need of a break with Kev limping sullenly behind them. Tiler was clearly not pleased about having been beaten four times.

'Don't worry, Tiler,' said Trev. 'It's just the type of game it is – fast and open. There'll be more goals in the next half; we just have to make sure we get the last word. You're all starting to let the ball do the work, which is why you're all still standing. Stick to it in the second half, and we'll get there.' There was no response as they stood sipping from their water bottles.

'Paul?' Trev said.

Paul was bent over with his hands on his knees and could barely speak. He just shook his head and gave a thumbs-up. Too soon, the whistle blew for them to take their places for the second half.

'Come on, guys; we can do this,' urged Bethan.

Trev was proved right. Within just three minutes, four goals had been scored, making it 7–5 to the Skunks. It had turned into a cracking game of football, with action at both ends and both keepers making frequent saves. Although they were tiring, the Ladz were thoroughly enjoying the game against their evenly matched opponents, and it was clear the spectators were too. Until the fifth minute of the second half.

After a save, Tiler rolled the ball out to Carl facing the goal in the right back position, and Carl trapped it simply, ready to pass it across to Paul at left back. As he turned towards the centre, he saw too late the smallest and quickest of the Skunks had spotted his plan and was in close, putting out a foot to intercept the pass. Carl's feet had nowhere to go, and his huge bulk headed for the hard floor as he tried his best to twist in the air and land on his back judo-style. He had managed to twist a little, but he took the fall on his shoulders, and his head whiplashed onto solid ground. The referee blew his whistle.

The little Skunk backed away, eyes wide. There were groans of horror from the crowd but silence amongst the players. After a few seconds, Carl started to move and, with help, got into a sitting position. 'Whoa, didn't see that coming,' he said groggily. He shook his head and started to his feet.

'D'you want to sit down a minute, Carl?' asked Trev.

'No, no, I'm fine. Let's just get on with it,' replied Carl.

'You're off,' said the referee.

'What?' said Paul, Carl and Trev in unison.

'You're off, mate. Head injury. We don't mess about with those here – there's no facility for an HIA, so you're off. Finito.'

'But …'

'No grey area, mate. Off. One minute to sort your team, Captain. Or concede. Up to you. One minute, and if we restart, it's a free kick to you.'

Carl walked unsteadily towards the gallery being helped, ironically, by Kev.

'What a fucking shitfest this has turned into!' said Tiler, throwing down his gloves.

Bethan said, 'I don't want to concede, not after coming this far.'

'I know what you mean, but maybe we should cut our losses this week,' said Gav. 'I mean, we were only just holding them with the full team, y'know? What chance have we got being short a player?'

'Thirty seconds,' the ref shouted across.

'OK, a quick vote,' said Paul. 'Those in favour— what the hell are you— Trev … what are you doing?'

Trev had appeared between Tiler and Bobby Brown. He was wearing Carl's football shirt.

'You can't—'

'I can and I am,' Trev replied. 'I'll just help out up front and stay out of trouble; don't worry.'

They all knew the possible consequences of a bad tackle on him, but he had clearly decided. Besides, there was no time as the ref had placed the ball.

'Starting the clock with five and a half minutes to go,' he said.

With that, they were underway once more.

Running more freely after the extended break, they started to put their game together, and with Trev distributing the ball from his position just ahead of the centre spot, the rest of the team were now playing further up the pitch. It was plain to see he was loving being involved. The Skunks could not get a foothold and, as they had been running around ball-chasing, they were beginning to tire.

Tiler was virtually on vacation as the Ladz pressed harder and harder. Inevitably, a goal came. It was an individual effort from Bobby Brown. After receiving a pass from Bethan on the right wing, he'd dribbled his way through a couple of defenders to toe-poke it perfectly into the bottom-right corner.

7–6.

Although the Skunks had the kick-off, in a couple of passes, Trev had the ball at his feet. He hit a perfectly placed pass to Gav who then attracted three Skunks. Once Gav got his pass away, it was a no-brainer for Bobby, who took the score to 7–7.

Paul was keeping an eye on Trev as best he could. It was like he had suddenly come alive; this was what he was on the earth for – his raison d'être. But Paul still worried that one slip or hard tackle would lead to a life-changing injury for Trev.

Then those worries left him as Bethan, running up the right wing, chipped the ball over a defender's leg to Trev standing some way back from the centre spot. It was such a perfect pass, not hard but hard enough, bouncing gently and exactly into his gunsights. Trev's face lit up as he eased back his right leg and struck the ball sweetly at the top of the bounce without spin. It seemed to happen in slow motion as the ball flew a foot off the ground, neither rising nor falling, through two defenders and Bobby Brown then past the motionless keeper, hitting the backboards with the crack of a handgun.

It was such an amazing, almost impossible goal, that all the players − Skunks and Ladz − turned to look at Trev. His eyes immediately reddened as players from both teams applauded him.

'Still thirty seconds to play,' said the ref, unmoved.

Shortly after the kick-off, the full-time whistle went, and the game was over. The Ladz had won, eight goals to seven. What a match!

The spectators gathered round the players. They had been captivated by the to-ing and fro-ing of the game, the injuries, the comeback at the end and, finally, by Trev's magnificent deciding goal. Both teams unusually stayed on the pitch discussing the great match and how tight it had been.

'Clear the pitch!' shouted a new referee. 'Next match to start in five minutes.' They all headed back to their tables.

'NO-HOPERS TO PITCH NUMBER TWO. LADYKILLERS TO PITCH NUMBER TWO. NO-HOPERS AND LADYKILLERS TO PITCH NUMBER TWO.'

'They're going to be League Champions tonight, bunch of pricks,' said the P.S.V. captain, who had been watching the Ladz' match.

'Well, I won't be rushing over to congratulate them,' said one of the girls from the Bankers. Everyone agreed.

Paul looked around. The Ladz were becoming a bit of a

focal point in the Centre, with many of their previous opponents standing around their table chatting with one another. He was with Paula and their boys who had loved watching and wanted to go home now to play football. Bobby had already disappeared. Gav was talking to the little Skunk. Bethan was looking at the pictures Liz had taken. Carl was declaring loudly to everyone there was nothing wrong with him, and he'd had much worse on the judo mat. Tiler appeared to be having a normal conversation with the Skunks' keeper. Poor Kev was standing with Carl, looking a bit sorry for himself as he massaged his hamstring.

'Did you get my goal, Liz?' asked Trev across the table.

'Well, I did,' she said, 'but the ball was moving so fast, you can hardly see it!' This got a huge laugh.

'I'll definitely have a copy,' he said.

'I won't!' said the Skunks' keeper, still laughing.

'Well, you should have one 'cause you didn't see it the first time!' shouted the Skunks' captain. Now everyone was laughing.

'Don't let the missus see it, Trev. You'll be banned for life!' roared Carl.

'She *would* go crazy, that's for sure!'

There was a slight pause in the conversations as a loud bang on the backboards heralded the No-Hopers' first goal.

'They shouldn't be allowed in our league,' someone said to nods all round.

Paul thought it was strange there were no sounds of applause or congratulation from the No-Hopers after the goal. They seemed to be completely devoid of emotion towards each other. Odd.

He was thrilled the Ladz had won such a tough game. It was a win they could take forward to the big match next week. Could that propel them into the final? Wishful thinking, surely.

'D'you think we should text Matti, Paul?' said Bethan, who had been unusually quiet all evening, no doubt still annoyed with herself about upsetting Gav.

'I was thinking that. I'll just tell him that if he wants any help, we're all available.'

'He'll need some counselling after that one; it was pretty bad from what they're saying.'

'Well, me and Ahmed are in tomorrow, so we might find something out about it then. Poor bugger.'

'Yeah. Hope he's OK; he's a lovely kid. Right, I'm just going to grab a drink, and then we're off.' She headed purposefully towards Stella's buffet bar.

Paul was about to speak to Trev but suddenly thought about Bethan. Was it all going to kick off? But when he looked across, Bethan was snatching her drink from Stella and giving Bobby a filthy look before turning on her heel to march back to the table.

'What was it like being back on the pitch, Trev? And that goal?' Paul asked.

'Amazing,' Trev replied. 'When that ball bounced towards me, Paul – honestly, Beth couldn't have set it up better – I couldn't resist it. All those years of sadness and disappointment, all the setbacks and frustrations, came out in that one shot.' Trev's voice was cracking.

'A catharsis?'

'Yeah – a catharsis. And it's a great feeling.'

'And a great goal – win, win!' They laughed together as Paul patted Trev on the back.

As they were all readying to leave, Paul said, 'Two quick things. First, let me know if you can't make it for the Cup match next week; second, I'll text Matti, see how he is and let you all know. How's the hamstring, Kev?'

He was still rubbing it carefully. 'Sore. I don't know why these things always happen to me,' he said sadly.

Tiler leaned towards him, so they were face to face and declared slowly, 'I'll tell you why. It's because you're a fucking prick!' This set them all laughing, except poor Kev.

'Oh, and Beth,' said Gav, 'be careful with the report this week. Make sure you get the names right.'

'No, you carry on, Beth.' Tiler was on a roll. 'I mean, who are we gonna take the piss out of otherwise?'

'Dismissed,' Paul said quickly.

*

As he was walking home, Paul received a text from Matti:

Sorry I didn't make it tonight. I didn't feel up to it after today. I hope you did well. My mum says I should take a few days off, so I'll be back later in the week. Hope I didn't leave you short.

Paul fired back:

Yes, we won, but we did miss you. We heard what happened, so just take it easy till you feel well enough to return. Everyone wishes you well. Let us know if you need anything.

We're all here if you want to talk.

Paul knew from personal experience it took a long time to get these kinds of events out of your head. For someone as inexperienced as Matti to walk into it unexpectedly and unprepared, it could be mentally devastating.

He wished the lad all the best.

Chapter Sixteen

The following morning, Paul and Ahmed found themselves on shift with Daniel, who had been involved in the incident the day before.

In a quiet spell, Paul asked Daniel what had happened.

'The whole thing was a mess from start to finish,' he said, 'and the controller didn't help at all. You probably heard that Matti was out with one of the mobile managers, looking at the junctions and stuff.'

'Who was that?' asked Ahmed.

'It was Ray.'

'Ray? He's the best of them.'

'Oh, yeah, no problems with Ray,' Daniel said. 'It's just where it went afterwards. I got the message from the train driver that he had hit someone on the footpath crossing behind the tip. He was really shaken up because this young lad had been looking right at him as he was approaching, doing about ninety. The driver hit the emergency brake, but there was no way he could've stopped in time, and this lad just kept looking at him – making no attempt to move – just standing there. And then, that noise all drivers dread, and it was done.'

'Oh, God – that's tough,' said Ahmed.

'Even though the driver hit the emergency brake, he figured they didn't come to a standstill for about five hundred yards. So that's when I got on to Control to organise attendance, and they mobilised the emergency services and got Ray on the move.'

'So, Ray told them he had Matti?' asked Paul.

Daniel nodded. 'Straight away, but they told him to make his way to the crossing as there was always the possibility this lad was still alive. Our people know the access points much better than anyone else; they said they'd get in touch with Gerry for advice or maybe get Gerry to pick up Matti. Anyway, they rang me back, asking if Gerry was in his office as his number was going straight to voicemail; I looked, but his car wasn't there. So, then I start ringing him, leaving messages; Gav is ringing him and texting him; Control are by now super-annoyed – we're all trying to raise him, but no joy.'

'Who was the controller?' asked Paul.

'Justin. He wouldn't make a decision. Kept putting it onto Gerry, who no one could raise. Then, after twenty minutes, Ray's arriving on site with Matti, and he's asking for guidance, but he's also aware he needs to get moving because of the albeit unlikely chance this lad has survived – been sideswiped or something.'

Paul nodded. 'It happens ...'

'So, with no guidance or assistance from anyone,' Daniel continued, 'Ray asks Matti what he wants to do. Matti says he'll go with him in case he can help the lad but obviously not having a clue about what he's walking into. Well, when they get onto the track at the crossing, there's just an explosion of blood and flesh, and they walk straight into it. Ray said it was like a scene from a Tarantino film – said he'd never seen anything like it.'

'Sounds truly horrendous,' said Ahmed.

'It was clear they were unable to help the guy, so Ray took Matti back up off the track to wait for the police, but the damage was done.'

'Yeah,' said Paul. 'You can't unsee those sights.'

'The emergency services started doing their bit, and fortunately the police had a spare PC, so Ray asked if she would take Matti home. And that's what happened. Really bad.'

As Daniel finished his story, the main door buzzed. Paul checked the camera – it was Ray. He released the lock.

Ray appeared around the corner of the screens. He was a tall man, well into his forties and always smart and upright. He kept himself well-groomed with close-cropped dark hair and still wore his sharply cut Viva Zapata moustache from his Army days. 'Hi, Paul. Ahmed, how's things?'

'All good, thanks, Ray,' replied Ahmed. 'Daniel was just telling us about yesterday.'

'That's why I came up.' Ray was standing in the shade at the back of the room. 'You OK, Daniel? You were getting it from all sides up here yesterday, weren't you?'

'A crazy day for sure. Must have been awful down there.'

'I'll say,' replied Ray. 'Fifteen years in the Army, and I never saw *anything* like that. The poor kid couldn't stop throwing up. I blame myself; I shouldn't have taken him.'

'You can't blame yourself in the circumstances, Ray,' said Paul. 'That lad may still have been alive.'

'Maybe, but the worst thing was we walked right into it. There was even blood on the gate, we were so close. It was everywhere. Blood, limbs, bone – the worst ever. Horrendous. I think people who stand in front of trains think they'll just fall down dead. If they knew what was going to happen, they might think twice.'

'They probably aren't thinking at all by the time they get to that stage,' said Ahmed, looking at the floor.

Ray nodded slowly. 'True.'

Paul knew these conversations could go on for a while. It was a type of purging of such difficult trackside experiences they'd all been through.

'So, that was when the boy started throwing up. I'm just glad the police had someone to spare who could get him home. She was young and new to the job too, so they were glad to give her a break. His mother was beside herself with worry after he phoned her, apparently.'

'It didn't help that Control was so unhelpful,' said Daniel. 'Not to mention Gerry—'

The door slammed, and Gerry charged round the corner, obviously highly agitated.

'What the fuck did you do yesterday, Daniel? It was a complete and utter shambles!'

'*I'll* tell you what he did,' boomed Ray, stepping forward from the back of the room. 'He worked his arse off while you were off on a fucking beano!'

Gerry took a step back, surprised at seeing Ray. 'I . . . I wasn't available for just a few hours, and all this kicks off. I've got the boss on my back because it took so long to clear; I've got the police on my back saying I should have been there for Sebastian, and I've got his mother screaming down the phone for letting him go. You realise this could end up as a potential claim against the company? And who's going to be at the sharp end of it all? Me! Every time you lot screw up, it's always me who gets it in the neck!'

'You should have been here to help the boy,' Ray said pointing directly at Gerry. 'You should have been here to send Daniel home and cover for him after he'd had to deal with all that.' He added slowly with a sneer, 'Where *were* you?'

'Never you mind where I was. It's none of your business.'

'You were AWOL. We know you weren't off because Control checked.' Ray was clearly enjoying Gerry's efforts to remove himself from the firing line.

'Control!' Gerry spluttered. 'I'll be speaking to them too.' He was clearly still trying to shift the blame.

'Good, because see that red phone? It rings them direct, so now's your chance.' Ray picked up the receiver and thrust it into Gerry's hand.

He had no choice but to make the call. 'Gerry speaking. Who's this?'

Brief pause at Gerry's end. 'You were working yesterday, weren't you?'

Another pause while the other person spoke.

'Never mind where I was. Tell me, what part of sending a trainee down to a fatality did you think was a good idea?'

Pause.

'You really fucked this up yesterday, Justin.'

Pause.

'I told you: it doesn't matter where I was. I was unavailable for a few hours; that's all you need to know.'

Pause.

'Don't you dare try and blame me – or my people – for this.' Gerry looked round for support, but everyone avoided his eye. 'They did everything right. It was you who had a simple decision to make, and you weren't even capable of that. If this goes all the way, I'll make sure you fucking hang!'

Short pause.

'Of course, I know these calls are being recorded!' Gerry shouted, the phone shaking in his hand. Daniel, sitting directly in front of the phone call, flinched each time Gerry hollered. 'That's why I'm telling you this; it was you who should have made arrangements for Sebastian. Now we've got a traumatised trainee who's gone sick, his mother who's beside herself with worry, and a possible claim against the company. And it's all down to you!'

Pause. Gerry's agitation now palpable.

'No, I'll see *you* in court!' he cried as he slammed down the phone. 'I fucking hate controllers. They sit up there in their ivory tower on their inflated salaries, and they do fuck-all. And it's the likes of me who has to cover for them. Well, fuck them this time. Fuck them!'

The final 'fuck them' was barely audible over the slamming door as Gerry marched out.

Nobody spoke for a second.

Ray's mouth was open wide. '*That* is a man on the edge of a precipice,' he said slowly.

'Yeah. And soon someone up here is going to push him right

over it,' replied Paul. 'He's been getting worse recently; you just can't talk to him.'

'Nobody would want to talk to him,' interjected Ahmed.

'I've never seen anyone melt down like that since I've been doing this job,' Ray continued. 'He's tidied himself up, though. Last time I saw him, he was in a grubby old suit that looked like it had come from a skip, and what had once been a white shirt.'

'Yeah – and you could always tell what he'd had for breakfast from the stains on his tie!' said Ahmed with a laugh, clearly trying to lighten the mood.

'Strange he won't say where he was, though,' said Ray. 'Anyway, I've got to go. Take it easy today, Daniel. Try and have a quiet day. And if anyone hears from the boy, tell him I was asking.' At the door, he turned. 'How's the football going, Paul?'

'Really good, thanks,' he replied. 'A sticky start, but we're into the Cup semi-finals. Everyone's training now. Some of us are losing a bit of weight, too, which is what I was hoping for. Improve our health a bit. Even Tiler's on board.'

'Tiler! Last time I saw him, he was like a big, wobbly jelly – a loud one!'

Paul laughed. 'Nothing worse than a big, loud, wobbly jelly! But to be fair, he's losing weight and has started on Couch to 5K, so watch this space.'

'You might have started something. The other ROCs are talking about your football team and improving their health. If you get to the final, I'll get a carload together, and we'll come down and cheer for you.'

'Great – we'll get the outfits and pom-poms for you!' Paul laughed. 'If you watch out for the newsletter where Beth does a weekly report, you'll be able to keep tabs.'

'Will do. I'll see you, guys,' Ray said as he left.

'Wow. They're all talking about the team, Paul,' said Ahmed.

'Great, eh? Perhaps next week we'll really give them something to talk about!'

*

The atmosphere in the ROC cleared as the week came to a close. It was Friday morning, and Bethan was working with Kev and Tiler. Since starting the job, she'd noticed how fatalities always affected the whole group, even those not involved, particularly when the item appeared in the news, revealing the personal tragedy that led that person to the railway line.

She had been extremely careful with the spelling of names in her write-up, and it went out exactly as she'd written it, together with the picture of Trev's amazing goal.

Gerry hadn't appeared for the rest of the week, which had also lifted the atmosphere.

Matti arrived for his first shift back, feeling better and ready to take up his training.

'How ya doin', pal?' Tiler asked straightforwardly.

'Glad to be back, tbqh,' replied Matti. 'Just been sitting around in my bedroom staring at Netflix and YouTube. But I've been down that road before, and I didn't want to go there again, so I thought I'd get back here. My mother said I should try and put Monday behind me. You know, move on.'

Tiler looked at him blankly. 'What the fuck is tbqh?' he asked, dismissing all else that Matti had said.

When the laughter had subsided, Bethan explained, 'It stands for "to be quite honest".'

'Well, fuckin' say "to be quite honest" then, otherwise no one's got a fuckin' scooby what you're talking about.'

'A scooby? What on earth is a scooby?' asked Matti.

'A scooby – as in Scooby-Doo – a clue!' explained Tiler with a huff.

'Ffs,' replied Bethan as Tiler returned to his desk, shaking his head.

Matti was laughing helplessly.

*

Paul was in later to help cover meal breaks. He spent some of his time going through the rosters to see who was or, more to the point, was *not* available for Monday. Kev and Gav would be missing out, according to the roster. Probably for the best for Kev. He said he was still having pain but using ice and heat to calm it down. With the League matches finished, this could be the Ladz' last game of the season. It was a shame they would both miss it.

Paul had been trying in vain to raise the Centre manager to find out which teams had qualified and who the Ladz would be playing. Just before he went home, he finally got through.

'So, the teams for the semi-finals are, in no particular order ...' The guy loved a bit of drama; Paul half-expected a drum roll.

'... yourselves, of course; the No-Hopers, as you would expect; the Sharpshooters and the Hammers. So, the three top teams in the League, plus you.' Paul felt slightly miffed by the manager's tone. 'And the draw is ...' During the dramatic pause, Paul was praying they hadn't landed the No-Hopers. *Get on with it.* '... First game: The FatLadz! versus ... the Hammers ... Second game: the Sharpshooters versus ... the No-Hopers. Here concludes the draw.'

Even though it was going to be a difficult road ahead with any of the three teams, Paul was relieved. 'The Hammers – don't know much about them. Sounds like it's going to be a rough game,' he said, picturing more injuries.

'Not at all. They're a proper team, as they should be because they all work together in the pig factory. Hence the name.'

Paul stifled a laugh. Clever.

'Game One at seven o'clock. Game Two straight after. Both on Pitch One. Twelve minutes each way. Make sure you're on time, or you forfeit the match.' And he was gone.

Paul put it on WhatsApp straight away and was preparing to leave as the shifts changed over when the door slammed. Surprisingly though, it wasn't the dreaded Gerry who appeared round the screens, but Gwynfor. He was unusually animated – agitated and annoyed, even.

'Who stuck this to the boot of my car?' he just managed to blurt out, his face red. His arm was high in the air holding up a large, pink, stick-on dildo. Very lifelike. The only one in the room not to turn round was Kev, who stayed in his seat, staring straight ahead.

'I'll have you, you little bass-tard, Kevin!' He spat the words out. 'Three days people have been banging horns and flashing lights at me – *three days*. I thought it was because I drive so slowly. Laughing and pointing, they were! Laughing and pointing! I'll have you, Kevin, you little bass-tard!'

Although Kev hadn't turned round, his bobbing shoulders gave the game away. The whole room by now had collapsed into laughter at the thought of old Gwynfor driving round for all that time with a huge, proud dildo stuck to the back of his car.

He slammed it into a bin. 'Little bass-tard!' he repeated.

'Not quite so little, I'd say,' quipped the newly arrived Carl.

'Don't *you* start, Carl boy. It's just a good job *Mrs* Jones didn't see the blasted thing – I don't know what she would have done with it!'

Nobody replied; they just laughed harder at the joke nobody dared say. Carl backed off dramatically as if Gwynfor might lash out. He clearly wasn't entering into the spirit at all. With no empathy or support, he dropped his bag to the floor and flopped dejectedly into his seat. 'I'll give you Clown Kev, you little bass-tard,' he said, as Kev stealthily grabbed his backpack and made for the door.

Paul walked down the steps in the early spring sunshine, still smiling and wondering what Kev would get up to next. He found Bethan just coming off her phone as she leant against her car.

'Not a bad shift, Beth.'

She laughed. 'There's never a dull moment when Kev's around, that's for sure!'

'Yeah. How's things with you?'

'Really good at the moment. Work's OK, Liz is happy, we've got Rhodes booked for July and we're enjoying the football.'

'Should be a good game on Monday. We've got a strong side out, and with Bobby back to full fitness, anything's possible.' Would she react?

She pursed her lips. 'Don't mention that prick,' she rasped.

'It's Stella at the buffet bar, isn't it?'

'Yes. And the one before – and the one before that.'

'Yeah. I mean, we're all annoyed about what he's doing, but you seem to be feeling it more than anyone else.'

She stared at her phone's blank screen. Paul wiped a speck of dirt off her windscreen, letting his words hang.

Eventually, she responded. 'It's true.' She sighed. 'Probably goes back to when I was a kid. My father was the same as him. And me and my sister saw my mum deteriorate over the years as she watched her family fall apart.'

'Oh no. That's sad.'

'I mean, well, we were a happy family until I was about eight. My sister, Katie, would have been around six and a half, so the same age difference as Bobby's girls. That's when I remember the rows beginning. I found out later it had always gone on, and Mum had tried to shield us from it, but she got to the stage where she couldn't take it anymore. She would confront him after she'd heard he'd been seen with this one or that one. He was very charismatic, brilliant with me and Katie. But he was a classic tall, dark and handsome man, and women couldn't help themselves; they just fell at his feet. And he took advantage of that – big time.'

'What happened?'

'By the time I was, maybe, fourteen, Mum was a wreck. It wasn't just his carrying on; it was the shame he brought on her amongst her friends and the neighbours. To be fair, she toughed it out for our sake, but it left her a basket case. Finally, she told him to go.

'I remember their final vicious row. Me and Katie were under the quilt in my bedroom holding each other so, so tight. The louder it got, the tighter we held each other. Then he came upstairs to say goodbye – neither of us moved, neither of us answered – and he was gone. Our father was gone. We cried. We cried and cried. And then Mum came up, and we all cried together in my bed until there were no tears left. The sadness – it was overwhelming.'

Tears welled in Bethan's eyes. Paul didn't want to upset her, and she probably didn't want to drag all this back to the surface, but it was obviously still there; maybe it always would be.

'Well,' she continued thoughtfully, 'it took a few years – quite a few years – but eventually, after a lot of heartache, we started to come through. Mum put her grief behind her and tried to address her feelings of failure. Then she started to feel better. She got a job, began to reclaim her self-respect, and friends and neighbours told her that throwing him out was the best thing she could ever have done and that she should have done it years before. She's still climbing a mountain, but she's happier and enjoying life.'

'What happened to your father?'

'No idea. Haven't seen him from that day to this, but I'm sure he's doing OK. Men like him, they never change – they promise everything and give nothing – they use and discard, then they take their lies and move on to the next one.'

'Yeah.'

'So, when I see Bobby Brown, I see my father. When I see his daughters, I think of me and my sister in my bed that night, holding each other so tightly, and when I see his wife, I see my mum. It brings that terrible sadness back to me to think of those two beautiful little girls going through what we did. Perhaps if someone steps in, he might change his ways.' Bethan's cheeks were wet with tears.

'Pity he isn't listening to this conversation, Beth. So awful for you.' In a spontaneous movement, he wrapped his arms around her. They stood for a few seconds.

'Thanks, Paul. Liz knows about it all, but this is the first time I've laid the whole thing out at once, so it must still be deep within. Anyway, we're getting through it. I'm OK now with Liz, and Katie's happy with her boyfriend, and she's still living with Mum. They both work in town and travel together in Katie's car. So, yeah, it's moving forward.'

'What the fuck are you two up to?' Tiler was coming down the steps. 'I saw it all. Paul, you dirty bastard; you're old enough to be her father, for God's sake. You're worse than Bobby Brown – it's disgusting!'

'On that note,' said Bethan, getting into her car half crying, half laughing, 'I'm going!'

On his way home, Paul thought about Bethan's story and how easily and quickly things can fall apart. He counted his blessings and thanked heaven he had been brought up in, and still had, a happy home.

Chapter Seventeen

I t was the day of the semi-final, and the WhatsApp group was alive with match talk. Everyone was looking forward to the evening, and Paul was pleased they were all approaching it feeling good and with no injuries. Kev and Gav were gutted to be missing the game. Kev was still injured, anyway, and Gav was struggling for time off, so they just had to accept it.

Paul arrived especially early to soak up the atmosphere. He'd already gathered his team's payments and approached the Centre manager to settle up in advance of the match.

'Good that you're prompt; surprising how quick the time goes before a game,' the manager said without looking up.

'Yeah, definitely,' replied Paul, distractedly watching the main door.

'This'll be your last game before the three-month break.'

Paul's head whipped round. 'Unless we win,' he replied flatly.

The Centre manager slowly raised his head and looked Paul in the eye. 'Over many seasons, I've seen teams like yours come, and I've seen teams like yours go. It's your last game,' he repeated coldly.

Paul left the manager to his accounts. 'Bloody cheeky bugger,' he muttered as he went to grab a table close to Pitch One.

As he threw his bag onto the table, Carl, Bethan and Ahmed walked through the left-side double doors, laughing, while Bobby and Stella arrived through the doors on the right. The laughter ended suddenly. All three stopped dead as Bobby, after the slightest of glances to his teammates, walked on ahead with Stella.

'Honest to God! He's got the skin of a rhino, that bloke,' said Carl as they reached the table.

Bethan said nothing as she dodged Paul's glance, but he could feel she was a pressure cooker about to explode.

He was just about to ask if they'd seen Andy, when he appeared silently from behind them and dropped his kit onto a chair.

'Please stop doing that, Andy,' Paul said, starting a little in surprise. 'You're going to give someone a bloody heart attack!'

With twenty minutes still to go, everyone, including Tiler, had arrived. The place was beginning to buzz, which was odd as there were only the two games being played. Paul figured something else must be on too.

'Can you go and get Bobby, please, Ahmed? Do it discreetly.'

Ahmed furrowed his brow at Paul but did as asked.

When they were all together, Paul began. 'Right, we're here in the semis, and we've got a good draw. The Hammers were third in the League, and our position didn't reflect the fact we're improving with every game. So, I'll go through the team, then Trev will take us through the game.

'Tiler's in goal, of course'—Tiler struck a strongman pose— 'Carl and Andy are our strongest defence, me and Beth'll start midfield, and Bobby, you do your stuff up front. That gives us Matti and Ahmed as reinforcements, so hopefully everyone will get a break. We'll need it as it's twelve each way on the big pitch, so we're going to be out there for a long time. Just pray we all stay uninjured this week!' They all nodded. 'Trev?'

'I just wandered over to have a look at these guys. They're big, solid fellas – probably from throwing meat carcasses around all day. We remembered last time about using the ball to beat the opposition, so this week we step it up a gear. Andy and Carl, as big as you both are, you're going to have your work cut out tonight. I suggest, for the first half, we play it from the back. Stay deep, support Andy and Carl with just Bobby up front. Get the ball up to him if you can. We'll see how that goes and review it at half-time.'

Paul added, 'Don't forget, we're here to enjoy ourselves, so remember what Shakespeare said: "Meet with success and failure and treat them both as one" – or something like that, anyway.'

The Centre had filled up, and many were making their way to Pitch One. 'Good luck tonight, FatLadz!' It was the captain of the Bankers. 'It's gonna be difficult, but you've attracted a good turnout.'

'Thanks. We'll give it our best,' Paul replied.

Wow! Paul realised all those people were there to watch *them*. Unbelievable! Liz, Paula and the boys had also arrived with Trev's wife.

'No cameo from you this week then, Trev?' piped up Carl.

'God, no! That would be a divorce for sure. She's still going on about it. I shouldn't have shown her the picture. She said she's only come down to make sure I don't do anything stupid!'

That gave everyone a laugh as they waited for their call. It soon came.

'FATLADZ TO PITCH NUMBER ONE. HAMMERS TO PITCH NUMBER ONE. FATLADZ AND HAMMERS TO PITCH NUMBER ONE TO PLAY THE FIRST SEMI-FINAL FOR THE CENTRAL LEAGUE CUP.'

'Jesus Christ,' said Andy, cowering over-dramatically under the power of the speaker system.

'Let's do it. We can win this!' Trev said.

Tiler was first to step out onto the pitch. 'Show time!' he shouted, jumping and heading an imaginary ball.

They went through their warm-up with Trev pushing the outfielders to pass more quickly – one touch where possible. Bethan was warming up Tiler in goal. Paul glanced over at the opposition. They really were a big bunch – none of them under six feet and solid. It was going to be a tough one.

Paul lost the toss, and the Hammers elected to kick off. Suddenly the referee was blowing his whistle for the start of the match. It was immediately clear that, although the Hammers were big, they were dextrous on the ball and worked superbly as a team. They were constantly threatening the Ladz' goal, but Andy and Carl were on form and held them off. Tiler was tested, but they were unable to get the ball past him. The story of the first half was one of attrition, each team trying to wear down the other. Bobby, frustratingly, found himself helping out in his own half for the first ten minutes, but then there was a breakthrough.

A short ball from Carl to Bethan gave her enough space to push it accurately into the Hammers' half past their last defender. Bobby didn't need an invitation; he was straight on it. His first touch put the ball perfectly onto his favoured right foot and, with total self-belief, he hit the ball hard just inside the right post. 1–0.

Paul felt the pressure drop. They had absorbed all that the Hammers had thrown at them in this first half and still come away with a goal. The final couple of minutes were uneventful as the war of attrition continued. As the ref blew the half-time whistle, Paul had made no substitutions, as he'd believed this was the best team of starters to wear down the opposition. And that's what they'd done.

There was applause for both sides as the teams swapped ends and the Ladz gathered in the goalmouth.

'Here's the thing,' said Trev. 'You've done the hard work. You've worn these guys out. I've been watching them. They're so big, they're struggling to turn. I reckon they've got two minutes left in them at the most. What I suggest, Paul, is that you take Carl and Andy off, get the fresh legs on and, after holding their charge for the first two minutes, push up the pitch, play in their half, and they're beaten. Job done.'

'No problem. Me and Beth'll move back and use the fresh legs in the middle.'

Paul wasn't totally convinced, but he bowed to Trev's superior knowledge. The short break was soon over. Ahmed and Matti took their places in the midfield, and Paul and Bethan lined up at the back with Tiler.

As soon as the whistle went, the Hammers dispossessed the Ladz after a poor pass from Bobby didn't reach Ahmed. They pushed down the right, and Paul blocked the shot, which bounced out to the centre. There was another shot; Tiler parried it, and Bethan trapped it on the left. Then they started putting some passes together – Bethan to Ahmed to Matti and backwards to Paul, who'd moved up to the halfway line. The Hammers were losing their organisation as their legs were tiring. Paul hit the ball hard through the centre, right to left, to Ahmed, who feigned a pass to Bobby as it came through. That forced the keeper the wrong way. Ahmed let the ball run and diverted it into the now open goal. 2–0.

It was a great move, possibly their best yet. The spectators applauded and cheered for the Ladz. After the kick-off, the Ladz soon had the ball back, and they passed it between themselves like a Premier League side. After that, there was little competition. The Hammers were exhausted, struggling to keep up with the Ladz, who were in complete control owing to Trev's idea of limiting their running. Two more goals for Bobby and an individual effort from the halfway line for Bethan made for a perfect score with a clean sheet at the final whistle. 5–0.

Paul was thrilled as the spectators started to spill onto the pitch. 'Well done, guys,' he shouted, but no one heard amid the clamour.

Trev approached him. 'Great game, Paul.'

'No. Great game, *you*. Your tactics were spot on. If we'd tried to run like they did, we would never have lasted the first half. Brilliant, Trev.'

'I must admit, the strategy worked well.'

'We're through to the final, Trev. This is amazing!'

Paul made his way to where the rest of the team were celebrating. It was a great moment as they all posed crazily for a picture for Liz. 'That will go with the report, for sure,' she shouted over the noise.

There were handshakes all round, the well-beaten Hammers taking their loss as good sportsmen. Players from many of the other teams were there to watch the semi-finals, and the whole thing was turning into a social event, with the Ladz at the centre.

'Well done, FatLadz!' someone shouted. It was Tiler, clearly thrilled with his clean sheet.

'Clear the pitch! Clear the pitch!' the Centre manager was shouting from the middle to no avail. Everyone seemed to have forgotten there was another match to play. He marched off.

'PLEASE LEAVE THE PLAYING AREA FOR US TO PREPARE FOR THE NEXT MATCH. I REPEAT: PLEASE LEAVE THE PLAYING AREA FOR US TO PREPARE FOR THE NEXT MATCH!' Some people covered their ears under the power of the tannoy that all but shattered their eardrums.

The Ladz got back to their table through the mêlée and sat for a short debriefing.

'Well done, everyone,' said Paul. 'That was the best thing ever out there, and now we're in the Cup Final!' There was whooping and high fives from everyone around the table. 'Trev?'

'I agree. You all carried out our plan perfectly. We won! And now we're through to the final!'

More whoopin' and hollerin'!

'No more to say,' he added.

Even more whoopin' and hollerin', high fives and laughter!

'THE NO-HOPERS TO PITCH NUMBER ONE. THE SHARPSHOOTERS TO PITCH NUMBER ONE. THE NO-HOPERS AND THE SHARPSHOOTERS TO PITCH NUMBER ONE TO PLAY THE SECOND SEMI-FINAL FOR THE CENTRAL LEAGUE CUP.'

'This is it, guys. This is when we find out who we're playing,' said Paul enthusiastically. It was only at that moment he realised they might be heading for a rematch with their nemesis, the No-Hopers. The idea was partly mouth-watering and partly disturbing.

'Everyone staying?' asked Carl.

Andy had to go home, and Bobby had already disappeared to his usual spot, but the rest made their way back to the pitchside.

Matti looked a bit down. Although he'd played well, Paul suspected it was because he'd had two, albeit difficult, chances but still couldn't get that elusive first goal.

Ahmed picked up on it. 'You're thinking about those chances, aren't you?' he said.

'Yeah. Can't understand it. I'm doing OK 'til I get in front of goal, and then I just, well, go to pieces.'

'Just a bit of stage fright – it'll all come together. Don't worry; that'll just make it worse. Y'know, although you didn't score, we couldn't have won without your work rate in the second half.'

Carl joined in. 'You just keep doing what you do, Matti. You don't have to score to have a great game.'

'I suppose,' mumbled Matti, unconvinced.

The Sharpshooters were already warming up, while the No-Hopers were ambling over from their table. Paul noticed that, as usual, none of the other teams interacted with them, and they made no attempt to interact either – even with each other. As they walked past the Ladz, one turned to the other. 'Twenty-three–nil, wasn't it?'

'Yeah,' his teammate sneered. 'A record, I believe!'

'Pricks!' said Carl, walking behind them, obviously not worried if they heard him or not.

The No-Hopers were so confident, they had no substitutes and were not bothered about a warm-up. There was a lot of shouting for the Sharpshooters, which died down as the No-Hopers made their entrance, walking into the sound of their own footsteps. They took their places with no ceremony and waited for the warm-up to end. There was no doubt in Paul's mind the whole spectator area wanted to see the No-Hopers dethroned, and they didn't care who did it. They had already taken the League, and nobody wanted to see them lift the Cup again with another one-sided final.

The game began with some to-ing and fro-ing, the Shooters trying to get in early with a driving attack up the middle. This was thwarted by an interception by the No-Hopers' captain. After some lightning-fast passing, the No-Hopers were ahead.

By half-time, the writing was on the wall with the No-Hopers 4–0 up, and they'd hardly broken into a gallop. People started to leave. They couldn't bear the thought of watching the No-Hopers cruise to such an easy semi-final win.

When the No-Hopers scored again with just a minute gone in the second half, Trev turned to the other Ladz. 'Have you seen enough?' he asked. Everybody nodded, and they made their way back to their table.

'Well, guys,' said Trev, 'we're in the final, and it's looking like it's going to be the No-Hopers. What d'you all think about that?'

'Bring it on!' said Tiler brashly, then quieter and more threateningly, 'Let me at the little fuckers!'

'We'll do our best; that's all we can do,' echoed Ahmed.

'We need some kind of game plan,' said Trev. 'I know those guys are a bunch of pricks, but they're pricks who are bloody good footballers.'

The Centre manager came over to speak to Paul. 'Well,' he said, 'that was the upset of the year so far, but you'll need more than an ace up your sleeve next week, that's for sure.'

Paul didn't answer.

'The final is at seven thirty next Monday evening. Fifteen each way plus five extra time and then penalties. So that we have no favouritism, we have an independent professional referee.'

'An independent professional referee?'

'Yes. We have to pay him, so tell your team subs will be up a bit. Admission is by ticket only, available in advance at the desk.'

'Tickets?' said Paul, confused.

'Yes. It's all-ticket. Only one pound. You'll be surprised how many turn up for this, and we're restricted to two hundred and fifty.'

'Two hundred and fifty?'

'Are you going to repeat everything I say? Yes. Most of the players from the other teams will be here, plus their partners and children. It's an end-of-season social event too, so tell your supporters to buy their tickets in advance and get here early. We put on food and drink with the ticket proceeds. It's a good night, but what people really want is to see that lot beaten. It's always a dampener when they're awarded the trophy after the match.' He was nodding towards the pitch as a slam on the backboards indicated another goal for the No-Hopers. Seven–nil, according to the scoreboard.

'We'll do our best,' said Paul.

'It won't be good enough,' the Centre manager said as he spun round and returned to the pitch.

As Bobby passed their table, heading towards the toilets, Paul became aware of a disturbance at the buffet. Bethan had obviously chosen her moment and was leaning over the counter, waving a finger at Stella. It was clear she wasn't there for a quiet chat.

Liz was editing her pictures, so Paul grabbed a surprised Carl and dragged him over. He'd had a feeling the tinder box was going to ignite tonight.

'… because we're all adults, sweetheart,' Stella was saying as Paul and Carl drew near.

'What about his kids? Those little girls – *they're* not adults, are they?'

'Well, you can't make an omelette without breaking a few eggs, dearie,' Stella sneered.

'No – but you can stop tearing families apart just for a quick screw in the car park!'

'I'm not going to be lectured on morals by a fucking dyke!'

'You fuckin' bitch!' Bethan's right arm drew back sharply, and her elbow caught the approaching Paul above his left eye.

A stabbing pain shot through his head, and he reeled back against a table, knocking over two chairs. Carl was behind him and managed to catch Bethan's arm before she started her swing. 'Come on, Beth. You can't be doing that; let's get back.'

Bethan took a bit of holding as Carl manhandled her, still shouting, back towards the table. With his free arm, he had picked up Paul, whose head was throbbing as warm blood trickled down his face. He didn't know whether to hold his head or his back. All this had gone unnoticed by most, as there was still a lot of noise coming from the spectators at the pitch, even though the Shooters were being well beaten.

When Andy saw Paul's eye, he grabbed some serviettes. 'What a mess,' he said, as Paul found a seat. 'You been fighting again, Paul?'

'I fell,' replied Paul pathetically.

Bobby Brown returned from the toilets, blissfully unaware of the altercation. As he reached the buffet, Stella pointed at Bethan, clearly telling him what had happened while he'd been gone. Bobby made a show of checking his watch as if he suddenly had to leave. But Stella gesticulated on, then stood back with her arms folded tightly, apparently waiting for Bobby to do something.

But they'd all seen it time and time again in Bobby's affairs – his modus operandi never changed. He'd spend as long as it took, whether days or weeks, to build the relationship towards the bedroom, but as soon as it turned from the physical to the emotional, he'd back off. He remained rooted to the spot.

Stella shouted at her assistant, who had witnessed the whole episode, that she was having an early finish. She grabbed her coat, walked past the table and glared at Bethan, who glared back.

Bobby, following her like a lapdog, picked up his bag, looked questioningly at Bethan and mouthed, 'Why?'

She drew breath to give out to Bobby, but Carl was quick. 'What did you think of the game tonight, Beth?' This was enough to distract her as she turned to look at Carl. When she looked back, Bobby was gone.

'Prick,' she said.

'Calm down. He's gone now, Beth,' said Liz, taking her hand.

Paul was glad to have got the inevitable over without too much fanfare. He didn't want their efforts negated by getting thrown out of the Centre for abusing the staff. He was still massaging his back, where the corner of a table had dug in, and holding a pad against his eye.

'Sorry, Paul,' said Bethan, calmer now. 'Really sorry. Hope it's not too bad.'

'I'm just glad Carl was there.' He tried to laugh.

'You've got the strength of an army in those biceps, Beth,' said Carl. 'And you'll have a black eye tomorrow, Paul. You'll be like Clown Kev; explain that to the missus!'

Their laughter spread to the rest of the table.

Eventually, Paul stood. 'Well done, everyone,' he said.

The final whistle in the second game interrupted him. It was obvious who had won, as there was little applause and no cheering.

'So, we're fortunate to get away with no injuries …'

'… except yours!' shouted Andy, to more laughter.

'… so, I think we'll have a full team available for next week. I'll have a look at the rosters to figure out how we can get all eleven of us off work at once. Let me know if you can't make it for any other reason.' He briefed them on the ticket situation. 'So, be prepared to make a night of it. Trev?'

Trev stood. 'Every one of you was brilliant tonight. No one took a backward step. Our game plans have been perfectly carried out, but I don't have to tell you that next week is a whole new level. I'll have a think through the week and try to figure out, firstly, how to avoid a twenty-three–nil drubbing and, secondly, how to win.'

'Anyone else?' said Paul.

'We're in the Cup Final!' shouted Carl, to the cheers of everyone else.

'Well done, everyone. Absolutely brilliant. Dismissed.'

*

'What on earth happened to you?' Paula said when Paul returned home.

She had left after the match so was unaware of any incident. She laughed when he told her. 'It's still oozing a little.'

'I hope I don't get a black eye,' Paul moaned. 'They laughed enough at Kev.'

'That Bobby Brown – he's terrible, isn't he?' she said. 'I often see his wife in town with the girls. She's so quiet, and the girls are so lovely. It's sad. Demeaning for her that everyone knows what he does, and she knows everyone knows.'

'That's exactly what Bethan was saying about her mother and how it all but destroyed her. Yeah – really sad.'

'Was everyone on a high afterwards?' Paula said.

'It was brilliant! And now we get to have a go at the No-Hopers again. I really hope we can do better this time. The only thing is, I think it's me who's on shift next week, so I'll have to find someone to work for me.'

'Can you do that?'

'We normally get by one way or another. I don't think we've had ten off, eleven including Trev, at the same time before, but it should be OK.'

'Come on. Let me put some butterflies on that, otherwise it'll scar.'

Chapter Eighteen

Liz had written a brilliant report, complete with photographs, which Bethan had sent for publication. Knowing their progress was being followed by the other ROCs gave the report an extra dimension for the team, and, by Wednesday, enquiries were coming in about attending the final. Ray had already organised his carload from the Eastern ROC, and Carl had directed him to the Centre, alerting him to the ticket situation.

Paul had been manipulating the rosters, trying to organise cover without Gerry's involvement. He arranged with the roster clerk that Samantha could cover Tiler, as she knew the area, and that Daniel would work his day off to cover Paul. That would mean all ten, plus Trev, had the evening off. Job done.

Coming towards the end of a quiet week in the ROC, Paul was pleased that all talk was of the final. He noticed Gerry had made no appearance to motivate the troops – in fact, he was notable only for his absence. Someone had made posters: *Come On, You FatLadz!* with a drawing of a super-fat Tiler filling the goal so no one could score. Fortunately, he'd seen the funny side and hadn't ripped them down.

Bethan and Bobby had worked a shift together, but she told Paul that they had given each other a wide berth. She explained she'd been exhausted after the match, physically and mentally, as these childhood memories were being unexpectedly stirred up within her, wearing her out. To ease things, she'd taken time to visit her mother and sister, but she hadn't discussed her thoughts with them, as she didn't want to disturb the memories and feelings they had – or at least appeared to have – put to bed. They told her she seemed distracted, but Bethan had told them she loved them dearly, and that was the reason she'd gone there. She told Paul they were puzzled, but she'd reassured them she was happy and looking forward to playing in this big football match.

Paul had worked every day and seen or spoken to the whole team. Bobby had actually been talking about the football. On shift with Paul and Carl, he said he was pleased with the way it was going. Without bragging, he told them he'd always been a goal-scorer; he just had the knack of being in the right place at the right time, so still scoring goals when he was well past his sell-by date felt good. Plus, this renewed fitness made him feel better than he had for a long time.

Carl agreed, saying how this newly found aerobic fitness was helping him with his gym work. Paul nodded as Carl told them he was thrilled because they were restaging the bench-press competition at the gym, and he was going to take part. He was out to prove he was clean and drug-free, which he always had been anyway. It was just a week away, but he was already fully fit, owing to the extra training he'd been doing for the football. He had not one ounce of unwanted fat. 'I can't wait,' he told them.

Trev said he was spending his week trying to figure out a game plan to live with the high-flying No-Hopers. He hadn't got as far as thinking the unthinkable – actually beating them. But he still had time; it was only Friday, after all.

Apparently, for fixing Andy's car, Ahmed wanted a radio-controlled U-boat that fired torpedoes while submerged, which his nephew had requested for his birthday. And a birthday card. Andy asked Paul, 'Where the hell am I going to get a radio-controlled U-boat that fires torpedoes while submerged?' Paul had no answer – he just smiled.

Kev was really cheesed off. His silly attempt at an overhead kick had torn his hamstring, and no amount of physio was going to get him ready for the final. He was still in a lot of pain but would definitely be there to support the team. Paul sympathised when Kev said, 'It's gonna be difficult though, just watching.'

Paul had also bumped into Gav who had managed to organise, through one of his contacts, some banners, flags and T-shirts sporting a quickly thought-up logo. It was very basic – a fat guy with a football for his stomach in a hastily drawn football stadium, with hands aloft in a victory salute, saying, 'Come on, you Ladz!' on a blue background. Gav wanted to sell them on the night, but Paul said he would pay for them out of leftover subs and to give them to anyone who wanted one. Gav was gutted; he had been hoping to make a small profit from the merch.

Matti was still affected by the incident on the tracks but told Paul he was settling down with the support of a counsellor arranged by the company and help from the Ladz and the rest of the ROC. He was disappointed Gerry hadn't even rung to see how he was, but at the same time he was pleased he didn't have to speak to him. He'd managed to get a ticket for his mother, and they were looking forward to the match.

Even Tiler seemed on a high. He pulled at his waistband to show how much weight he'd lost since their exploits had begun. 'Look, Paul. Eighteen pounds gone!' he gushed. Paul had asked him how he was getting on with his training.

'Loving the football – great to be back doing something physical – and the Couch to 5K group have nominated next Saturday morning's Parkrun as our first full-distance effort.' He confided in Paul that, apart from making a clubload of new friends, he had a running buddy – a woman of his own age who actually seemed to like him!

Paul was pleased. His efforts had come to fruition. All in all, there was a good feeling around the place. The players were all better physically – with the possible exception of Kev – and mentally, and their pending meeting with the No-Hopers was making the ROC bubble and fizz. Even non-players were on board, discussing with Trev and Paul possible ways to win the Cup Final.

Those who were playing, though, were just hoping Trev could come up with something by Monday.

Chapter Nineteen

Paul had worked the Sunday night shift, but he was up by one o'clock. He immediately posted on the WhatsApp group: *It's Monday! Who's up for a football match?*

Everyone had replied within half an hour as he was eating his breakfast, all of them clearly thinking of nothing else. Carl, Andy, Kev and Matti were in work but would be finished in plenty of time. Paul gave Paula her tickets, threw his kit in the car, picked up the practice balls from the garage and prepped his sports drink. He wanted to do things as he thought of them to make everything go as smoothly as possible. He and Paula were chatting at the sink while they washed a small backlog of dishes.

'I should tell you – I saw Bobby's wife, Tasha, in town yesterday,' said Paula.

'How is she?'

'A bit withdrawn. It must be difficult, knowing that, well, people are talking.' She paused. 'I think I might have made a bit of a booboo.'

'What d'you mean?'

'I wasn't thinking; I just said it.'

'Said what?'

'I said how well the team had done to get to the final of the Cup, and how great it was going to be on the night, and about Bobby scoring all those goals.'

'And?'

'She didn't know anything about it.'

Paul stopped wiping a plate. 'Bugger.'

'Exactly what I thought. Then she asked for details, so I told her when it was. I think she was interested in getting tickets for her and the kids.'

'Double bugger,' said Paul. 'Well, you couldn't lie to her, and we can't sort out their relationship – that never goes well. Anyway, she might not even go.'

'You're probably right. Bobby's put everyone in such a difficult position.'

'So true,' he replied as he finished drying the last dish.

Paul put one more post on the group: *We'll do our best tonight, but it's going to be a great atmosphere, so whatever happens, let's enjoy it!*

It was soon surrounded by emojis agreeing and liking. Nothing from Tiler's Nokia 3310, of course.

*

Paul had just parked up on the school run. He was half an hour early, so he set his alarm and relaxed back to have a doze. He was completely chilled, the football pushed to the back of his mind. After three consecutive night shifts, he was asleep immediately, his head supported on one hand against the window.

But there was a disturbance. So deeply had he fallen, he had to look around groggily to remember where he was. As his brain came slowly back to life, he realised his phone was ringing. He checked his watch – he'd only been sleeping for ten minutes. He grabbed his phone from the passenger seat. Gerry. What the—? Was he ringing to congratulate the Ladz for getting so far and wish them luck in the final? No way. So, what *did* he want?

Paul answered warily. 'Hello?'

'It's Gerry.'

'I know.'

'Right. You've got to work tonight.'

'What? No. It's all sorted. Sam's coming in to cover Tiler, Dudley's working his shift and Daniel's covering me!'

'It's all fallen apart,' sneered Gerry. 'Daniel just rang. His daughter's had another attack; he can't come in.'

Paul's heart was pounding. 'But—'

'I think he's lying again. Says he's at the hospital – I couldn't hear anything medical going on.'

'But we've got the final tonight …'

'You've got no choice. It's your shift, and there's no one else. You're the last man standing. I'm far too busy tonight to do anything.'

Paul knew Gerry was right, but his mind was working overtime to think of a solution. All he could manage was a weak, '… but the football—'

'Football, football, football. That's all we've had for these last months. Fuck the football. Everyone's fed up to the back teeth with it!'

Paul tried to keep calm. Gerry was enjoying this too much. 'Is there no …'

'There's no one! It's your shift. Be there and be on time!'

Paul took a breath to speak, but the phone was dead. Gerry was right – it was Paul's shift, and it was down to him to ensure it was covered. Gerry was also right that there was no one else. It was always going to be difficult to get all ten players plus Trev off at the same time, but he had never envisaged a situation where he would be the one to miss out.

He was distraught and deep in thought when a text came through from Daniel:

Hi Paul. Really sorry I have to let you down. I'm in the hospital with Emily and she's really struggling this time. We're just hoping for the best. Sorry once again.

Paul never for one instant suspected Daniel was lying as Gerry had suggested, and, for a moment, Daniel's message put things into perspective. He sent Daniel a supportive text and put the whole thing to the back of his mind as he waited for the boys to come out of school.

*

When Paul arrived back at the house, he couldn't help hanging his head. He had left the house without a care in the world, but when he'd returned, he felt he had *all* the world's cares on his shoulders.

He explained to Paula what had happened, and she squeezed his shoulder. He was going to be stuck in work when he should be leading the team out in the Cup Final. He'd already put his kit, his bottle and the balls into his car, and he'd been more excited than ever.

He started to type a post on WhatsApp, but it was difficult to find the words. Eventually, he decided to make it short and sweet – well, short, anyway: *Bad news, I'm afraid, guys. Gerry just rang to say that Daniel has had to go to hospital with his daughter and can't work tonight. As it was my shift and there's no one else, I have to go in. I know you'll all be brilliant – just a shame I can't be there.*

The replies started coming in immediately. Everyone was sympathetic to Daniel but gutted for Paul. Carl suggested asking Gerry, but Paul explained Gerry said he was too busy to help, and he thought little of their efforts anyway. They couldn't believe it, but they knew there was no room for manoeuvre.

'You still go,' he said to Paula. 'I got the tickets for you, and they're like gold dust.'

'Yes, I will, as they all make a fuss of the boys, and the boys love Bethan and Liz. They'll still want to see the final.'

'Can't believe it; thought I'd covered everything. I thought I had everything sorted.'

'You can't think of every eventuality.' She sighed. 'I'm trying to think of something positive to say here.'

'I know, love. Thanks for trying, anyway.'

*

Paul parked his car outside the ROC. He still couldn't believe this was happening. He slammed his door and walked thoughtfully up the steps. His heart rate didn't even rise, and he wasn't panting at the top of the steps.

He was so much fitter than he used to be, but it was to no avail. He'd never felt this devastated. Even though he told himself he was over-reacting, he couldn't let it go. After all he'd achieved: getting the team off the ground, coaxing everyone to carry on after such a terrible start, organising the training, getting Trev involved and turning them into a credible and popular team that had now qualified for the Cup Final. No matter how many times he told himself it was just a game of football, he was distraught, and that feeling wasn't going to go away anytime soon.

He arrived early to give Kev plenty of time to hand over and leave in time for the match. Matti had already gone, but Carl and Ahmed patted Paul on the back with doleful expressions of sympathy. Paul threw the practice balls to Carl, wished them luck and told them to listen to Trev. 'Take it to the No-Hopers, Ladz, and text me when it's over.'

Ten minutes later, they were on their way, and Paul was set to face a miserable night shift. Dudley made him a cup of tea. Sam chatted to him for a bit, trying to lighten his mood, but he just wanted to be left alone. There were no problems, so the railway pretty much ran itself. The atmosphere became subdued, subsiding into a peaceful calm as they monitored their sections.

Chapter Twenty

There was still an hour to go before kick-off, but Trev wanted to arrive early in case he needed to parry any negativity after Paul's unexpected withdrawal.

As he walked into the Centre, he was surprised to see tables had been arranged for the teams and their supporters. On the far side close to the pitch, a table was adorned with a grand black sign neatly inscribed with the No-Hopers' golden logo. At a table nearer the bar and buffet, a similar sign in blue stated *The FatLadz!* There were freebies on each team's table: bags, energy bars, drinks, keyrings and assorted sports paraphernalia. It was quiet, except for the soft hum of the aircon. A local sports reporter was chatting to the Centre manager.

As he settled at the table, Trev was pleased to see the team weren't far behind him. Bethan and Liz were first, then Andy, Carl and Kev arrived, deep in conversation. Matti came next, with his mother and his new girlfriend, who Trev had learned from gossip was Michaela, the young police officer who'd taken him home on that awful day. Following behind was Paula, looking a bit down, with her boys, and then Ahmed and Gav, complete with partners and children. Bobby Brown made his appearance, shamelessly walking in with Stella. Trev was worried for an instant when she and Bethan exchanged glances, but Bethan looked away immediately, having promised Paul and Trev that she wouldn't get involved this week.

Finally, Tiler arrived. Although he was last, he was not late, so that was an improvement, but more noticeably, he was holding hands with a lady.

'What the—?' said Kev. 'Tiler's got a girlfriend?'

They all looked across as Tiler approached with a smart, middle-aged, auburn-haired lady in a powder-blue tracksuit and pink trainers. 'You all waiting for me?' he grinned. 'This is Claudia. Claudia, these are my colleagues.'

They were a bit lost for words but quickly welcomed her. 'Good luck tonight, everyone,' she said in a pleasant Home Counties accent. 'George has told me what you've all been through to get here.'

More silence ensued while they processed hearing Tiler's first name used by, well, anyone, really. Trev noticed Matti's puzzled expression; the lad clearly had no clue who she was talking about!

'Great,' replied Trev, taking the reins. 'We're all here nice and early, so I just want to say, well, I don't want us to begin on a downer, but, how unfortunate it is the way things have turned out for Paul.' Everyone was nodding. 'We all know this is his baby and, without his organisation, right now, we'd all be at home in front of the telly with a pizza and a bottle of plonk. So, putting a positive slant on it, let's do our very best tonight, continue our improvement, and try and get a good result. Let's do it for Paul.'

There was an impromptu round of applause for the absent Paul.

'We're really early. I suggest we take some time to drink in the intensifying atmosphere, build yourselves up in your own way and prepare for the fray. Meet back here in twenty minutes, and we'll get down to it.'

Trev was right about the atmosphere building up. The volume was rising as more people arrived and the tables filled up. He recognised some of their previous opponents coming in with their families and teammates. He'd seen Ray arrive with his carload of mates from the EROC and he was sure this was going to be a big night, which made him all the sadder for Paul missing it all.

However, Trev was determined to do his best and support the team however he could. They'd all worked so hard for it.

The atmosphere continued to ramp up as the minutes ticked by. Cup Final night. People were busy getting drinks in, children were running around freely and noisily, buffet food was being brought out to the tables, and the place was alive with activity. Stella had some helpers in but was still rushed off her feet, so Bobby Brown was not in his usual place. Trev could see him near the front desk chatting happily to Gav and Kev, when the conversation suddenly stopped and Bobby stiffened, looking straight ahead.

Trev became worried when Kev waved his hand in front of Bobby's face a couple of times; he could see him asking Bobby if he was OK, so Trev stood up to get a better view. Then he could see the reason for Bobby's change in behaviour.

At the doors, a woman stood with two young girls beside her. Kev and Gav soon caught on as they exchanged glances and retreated quickly to the table. They all watched as Bobby edged forward then looked back in shock. If he was seeking help, he was wasting his time.

'I really thought Bobby was having a stroke,' said Gav.

'Me too, but all I could think was, who's going to replace him up front,' replied Kev.

'Well, he's made his bed, now he's got to lie in it,' said Trev.

Everyone was returning to the table for Trev's talk. Bobby was last to arrive, but no one passed comment.

'So,' started Trev, 'we've made it this far, and now it's time to ramp it up to elev—'

'Look!' shouted Ahmed, who was standing up and pointing excitedly at the doors.

They all turned towards the entrance.

*

The atmosphere in the ROC was in stark contrast to that of the Football Centre. It was dismal. Sam and Dudley had clearly given up trying to talk to Paul, whose thoughts were elsewhere. He was still trying to figure out if he could have done something differently to prevent this situation, but he kept drawing a blank. There was nothing he could do now, anyway.

He sighed. He was annoyed. He was sad. He was angry with Gerry who could have covered for an hour or two.

He looked at his watch as the door slammed. *Oh no. I really don't need this now.*

Gerry appeared around the corner. 'Oh, you *are* here, then?' he sneered as only Gerry could sneer.

Paul glared at him, determined not to bite.

'D'you know what? You people think you run this place, and you can just come and go as you please. Well, I'm gonna change all that. You think you've got a free hand? Think again. In future, I'll decide who works, when they work and when they don't work. Eleven people off at the same time? It's bullshit. Unacceptable bullshit!'

Paul's insides were beginning to boil.

Gerry persevered. 'I'm going to draw up a roster that will stop the Daniels and the Pauls screwing up the whole system. Daniel pretending to be in the hospital? He's nothing but a liar. You want a football team? Go somewhere else. The only staff I want here are those who want to work for me. They come in, stay quiet and piss off home without a fuss. There's no place for all this—'

Paul's rage bubbled over. 'Gerry. Why are you such a twat?'

Dudley's head dropped into his hands as Gerry gaped. 'What—what do you mean?'

'Have you looked around when you come in here? Have you seen the effect you have on people? Normal people. I'd say there's not a single person up here who could think of one positive comment to make about you.' It had been festering a long time; Gerry had it coming.

'Did you know everyone up here hates you?' Paul continued.

'That is, for clarity, we don't dislike you; we actively hate you. When you come in, slamming the door completely unnecessarily, heads drop, comments are made, and nobody speaks until you're gone. Nobody respects you because you're the worst and most useless manager we've ever had.'

'That's not true. I get on well with most—'

'Are you serious?' Paul's face warmed. 'Are you *serious*?' His voice broke as it rose. 'What about poor Daniel? D'you get on with him? Struggling with his seriously ill daughter, and all you can do is call him a liar. Is that getting on well with—'

'I do get on with people … you don't know …' Now Gerry's voice was breaking.

'I don't know what? How you treat everyone like shit? How you put the fear of God into poor Ahmed with your rants? Well, maybe *you* don't know. Maybe you don't know how much you're despised, detested and dreaded up here. Yes, people dread your—'

'You don't know what I'm going through. Nobody does. You're all so wrapped up in your own little bubble in here, you can't look out to see what's happening in the real world. Whenever I come in here, you're all so negative towards me. Not one of you has ever asked how *I* am!' shouted Gerry, his voice cracking.

'You? Nobody ever asks *you*?' Paul shouted. 'Nobody can have a conversation with you. You can't open your mouth without belittling or berating someone. So, nobody gives a flying fuck what you're going through – not a flying fuck!'

'But …'

'Go on, tell us. Tell us what you're going through that makes you such a horrible bastard to everyone you come across. Tell us! Tell us why anyone should have any sympathy towards such a self-centred psychopath who makes everyone's life such a misery, 'cause I wanna hear it. We all wanna hear it. Come on – we're all ears!'

Gerry's shoulders slumped. He was silent for a few seconds. 'I … I'm gay,' he said quietly.

Sam's glass smashed on the floor.

Paul stood silently, the wind taken out of his sails. 'What?' he said.

'I'm gay.'

'You're … *gay*?! Is … is that what … is that what all this is about?' Paul said in a less angry tone.

Gerry was staring at the floor like a naughty child.

'Because you're gay … and because you can't deal with it, you're trying to make everyone … *hate* you?' Paul was struggling with his own reasoning. 'Is that it?'

'Things are just … difficult,' Gerry replied in a faltering voice. He looked up at Paul with red eyes.

'This is crazy.' Paul paused. A few things slipped into place: Gerry's long absences, not answering his phone when they really needed him, his clandestine meetings, his aggression. It was difficult to have sympathy after all that had gone before, but Paul reached deep. 'The company can help you with that sort of stuff; it's no big deal nowadays.'

'With a wife and kids, it is a big deal. I don't know … I don't know what I … it's d-difficult …'

Paul spoke gently. 'Have you got a lov— a partner?'

'It's Lawrence.'

'What? Leering Larry the Lecher?'

'Don't call him that; you don't know him.'

Gerry was beaten down, his double life exposed. Paul felt defeated; he had nothing else to say. Sam and Dudley's eyes were as big as saucers.

Gerry walked past Paul and sat in front of the screens. 'Go,' he said.

'What?'

'Just go,' Gerry repeated.

Paul stared at Gerry, worried about leaving him in charge. He looked across to Sam and Dudley, who both nodded. He grabbed his stuff to leave.

'Paul?' said Gerry.

'Yeah?'

Flatly, with no emotion, he said, 'If you win, take the night off.'

Paul nodded slowly, checked his watch, then raced out the door and skipped down the steps.

Chapter Twenty-One

Paul ran into the Centre with his bag flapping open behind him, grasping his football shirt like a superhero about to change. There was an impromptu round of applause from the team, then fist bumps and high fives all round.

Carl shouted above the din, 'What happened? How d'you get out?'

Paul took a deep breath but paused. 'Too complicated – I'll tell you all later. Let's do this!'

Paula spotted him, and the boys came rushing over to greet their dad, beaming all over their faces. Their mum waved and called them back, as the spectator area was filling up fast. Paul could see that she'd teamed up with Bobby's wife and the two girls, who, along with Paul's boys, seemed to be tuning into the excitement of the night.

With only ten minutes to go before kick-off, the place was full and the atmosphere intense. The No-Hopers had arrived to no fanfare; they sat at their table tapping on their phones or fiddling with the freebies, apparently oblivious to all that was going on around them. One of them had swatted the sign off the table amid howls of laughter from his teammates, and it lay broken on the floor. A few of their guests stood nearby, clearly wondering what all the fuss was about. Much to the amusement of the Ladz, Bethan had given each No-Hoper a name: the Captain, the Goalie, the Obnoxious One, the

Really Obnoxious One, the Weird One and the Idiot.

'It's so obvious which one is which!' Ahmed said.

'Did you manage to give out all the banners and T-shirts and stuff, Gav?' asked Paul.

'Yes,' replied Gav a little sulkily.

'He was hoping to sell them,' explained Ahmed.

'Unbelievable,' groaned Tiler, shaking his head.

'Don't start, you two,' pleaded Trev. 'Just stand there and listen.'

Kev was the only one sitting down by now.

'It's great that Paul's made it,' Trev began, 'as now we're running with three subs. Let me tell you, we're going to need every second of running from all of you just to live with these guys, never mind beat them. The final is *fifteen* minutes each way, and that's constant. There's five minutes each way extra time, then penalties. Don't even think about that. We can't let it go into extra time – I think we all know we're not physically capable. We've got to give everything in normal time; that's the only way we can hope to stay with them.'

The team hung on to Trev's every word, knowing they had a mountain to climb.

'Concentration when you're tired is challenging, but we need to be on it if we're going to avoid a hammering. I've thought long and hard about this, and I think our tactic in the first half is to defend, defend, defend. I know it sounds negative, but it's partly energy-conservation and partly to frustrate them. If you get the ball, don't be tempted to break. Kick it upfield into a corner away from the keeper, so they have to go back to retrieve it; that'll give us respite. Bobby, I know you want to be scoring goals, but you'll have to bide your time. See where we are at half-time.'

'What? You gotta be jok—'

'No. I've thought this through.' Trev pushed on. 'Any other game plan eats into their hands and will only end with us tiring quickly and losing badly. Remember, we've worked hard to be here tonight, and we're not going in as sacrificial lambs. We're really in with a chance of winning the Cup Final! Paul?'

'OK, so we all know where we stand with this. I think the best team of starters for this will be: Tiler in goal, of course, Carl and Andy at the back, Beth and Gav in the middle, and Matti up front. But, going with Trev's game plan, everyone is to stay back unless there's a one hundred per cent chance of getting up there with a clear and safe shot on goal. Matti, you've got to run those legs into the ground tonight. Tiler, remember to keep your size tens inside that line – no penalties tonight. I'll call the changes as people tire. Remember, we're here to enjoy ourselves. If we lose, so be it, but at least we'll have given one hundred per cent.'

'What was that Shakespeare quote, Paul?' asked Andy.

'Oh yeah. He said: "Meet with success and failure and treat them both exactly the same."'

'It wasn't Shakespeare.' There was a pause, and everyone looked at Kev.

'What's that, Kev?' said Andy.

'It wasn't Shakespeare. It was Kipling. Rudyard Kipling. "If you can meet with Triumph and Disaster and treat those two impostors just the same, yours is the Earth and everything that's in it, and – which is more – you'll be a Man, my son."' Everyone, including Paul, stared at Kev silently at this unexpected display of intellectual prowess. 'His poem, "If"; we did it in school,' he said, his cheeks reddening.

Tiler broke the silence, 'I preferred Shakespeare's version,' which started them all off laughing and relieved some of the pressure of the night.

'FATLADZ TO PITCH NUMBER ONE. NO-HOPERS TO PITCH NUMBER ONE. FATLADZ AND NO-HOPERS TO PITCH NUMBER ONE FOR THE LAST MATCH OF THE SEASON. IT'S THE CUP FINAAAAAL!'

As the decibels of the Centre manager's voice rose towards the end, some of the children looked close to tears. There were only a few people around the tables now; most were in the spectator area which ran the length of the pitch on one side.

'Let's get in there,' said Trev.

Carl picked Kev out of his chair by the neck of his jacket with one giant arm.

'Show time!' growled Tiler.

'FIRST IN, IT'S THE NO-HOPERS!' boomed the tannoy. There was little spectator response as they wandered in wearing their red strip, the game no doubt already won in their eyes. First in was the Captain, followed by, as Bethan had christened them, the Obnoxious One, the Goalie, the Really Obnoxious One, the Weird One and, finally, the Idiot.

'FOLLOWED BY THE FATLADZ!'

The crowd – and by now it *was* a crowd – went wild with their banners and flags, shouting and clapping as the team walked in. Paul led them onto the pitch. How close he had come to missing the whole thing. From the pitch, the spectators looked like a sea of people – a huge crowd for such a small venue. Carl threw down the practice balls.

'Two minutes,' said the referee, setting his watch.

The No-Hopers were just messing around by their goal, but Trev made sure every one of his players took those moments seriously. He made use of the opportunity to motivate them, get them warmed up and give them a feel for the ball. Soon the ref blew his whistle and the warm-up was over. Paul went to the centre for the coin toss, which he was pleased to win.

'We'll kick off,' he said. He didn't want a repetition of their first start with the No-Hopers, that was for sure. Paul had decided on a curt handshake, but the Captain held on to Paul's hand and looked intently into his eyes.

'Twenty-three–nil, wasn't it? A record, I believe,' he said smarmily. With a sickening smirk, he turned and strutted back to his team. The jibe was lost on the referee, so Paul, simmering, left the pitch to join Trev, Ahmed, Kev and Bobby front and centre of the crowd.

There was another reason Paul didn't want to be in the starting line-up. He couldn't remember the last time he'd lost his temper, and he hadn't recovered from his altercation with Gerry. He thought it a good idea to take another ten minutes before he joined the fray.

The referee placed the match ball in front of Matti and Gav. There were cheers from the crowd as the Centre manager started the countdown.

'FIVE, FOUR, THREE, TWO, ONE.'

The whistle blew for the start of the Cup Final.

It was immediately apparent it was going to take a mammoth effort from the Ladz to not go the way of the No-Hopers' five previous Cup Final opponents. It was impossible to keep any kind of possession. The No-Hopers attacked like a swarm of bees so quickly, they couldn't be pinned down or marked. So, the Ladz stuck to the plan of holding back each raid through sheer weight of numbers, while trying to push the ball upfield to relieve each onslaught. Tiler was making amazing efforts to keep out any shots that got through.

Keeping the No-Hopers from scoring for the first eight minutes was a massive achievement, but then the inevitable happened. The No-Hopers pushed hard down the right, and too many Ladz went across to cover. This left the Idiot in space on the left. A perfectly placed ball shot through a gap from the Obnoxious One, and the Idiot made it 1–0.

The Ladz were gutted, so Paul took the opportunity to make some changes. He and Ahmed replaced Gav and Bethan who, like Matti, had not stopped running, but he resisted the urge to bring on Bobby. Bobby was the worst spectator ever. He was jumping around, wanting to get on the pitch and do what he did best. But Paul wanted Bobby to come on hungry. Hungry and angry.

The crowd was a little subdued by the No-Hopers' goal, but they urged the Ladz on as the attrition resumed. More attacks kept coming, but they were thwarted by all six Ladz vigorously defending the goal. They blocked with a foot here, a leg there, a knee – anything that disrupted and frustrated the No-Hopers as the minutes ticked by.

Matti found the ball at his feet on the edge of the area and, seeing a gap, he couldn't resist having a run to get that elusive first goal. Unfortunately for him, the Really Obnoxious One had drifted back and easily dispossessed Matti just past the halfway line, leaving Matti way out of position. The Really Obnoxious One sent a straight ball clean through the hole that Matti had left in the defence as the Captain ran into the centre. Then, with his back to the goal, the Captain used the speed of the pass to chip the ball over Tiler's outstretched hand, which was left groping at the air. 2–0.

Matti looked sheepish.

'Keep your chin up, Matti!' came a shout from the crowd. The spectators were noisily appreciating the efforts it was taking to keep the No-Hopers out, but Paul suspected, deep inside, they were thinking the writing was on the wall. Paul used the short break to take Matti off. Matti saw it as a punishment, but Paul reassured him it was because the Ladz would need all his running for the second half.

Bobby tightened his laces but looked up in surprise when Paul ran across and called Bethan back on. 'What the hell?' shouted Bobby angrily.

Paul didn't reply. Trev kept his eyes on the pitch.

After two minutes of fruitless attrition, the ref's whistle went for half-time. There was no doubt the No-Hopers were becoming frustrated by their inability to score at will, being used to leading easily going into the second half. But there was also no doubt that all the running was taking its toll on the Ladz.

As the team changed ends, Trev approached Paul. 'Carl and Andy haven't got much left.'

'I know. I just wanted them to get us through the first half and a couple of minutes into the second after a rest.'

Trev addressed his team. 'You're doing amazingly well. I know it's tough, but it's going to get tougher as we tire. We can really do this. We're just two behind, which this bunch are not used to, and they're getting frustrated. No one's ever taken it to them before. No one's rattled them, and that's what we've got to do in the second half. Tiler, you're doing really well, but now we need to make sure we don't give them early hope. If we can hold out for the first few minutes, we'll change up a gear and try to rattle them more. One thing to remember is that we must give everything this half. Don't even think about extra time; whether we like it or not, we haven't got the fitness or firepower to get through it. Paul?'

'Trev's right. While you're on, give it your all – no regrets when the final whistle goes. Also, I've been watching them; they've got no team spirit.' Everyone looked over to the No-Hopers, leaning on the goal or wandering around, killing time before the second half. 'I don't think they even like each other. This is the time to put them under pressure, to make them realise they're not the only team out there. As Trev said, "rattle them". OK?'

The whistle blew for the teams to prepare for the second half. As they walked out, Paul spoke quietly to Carl, who nodded as Paul walked away.

The No-Hopers stood ready for kick-off. The whistle blew, and the Captain touched the ball to his left as Paul suspected he would, trying the same move that gave the No-Hopers their instant goal in their first meeting with the Ladz. But Paul had second-guessed him, and as the Idiot came flying through, taking the ball with him, Carl stepped out from behind Paul. The Idiot hit a brick wall. He bounced off Carl cartoon-like, amid screams of foul play, but the referee shouted to play on. The crowd erupted. If the Ladz were going down, they would go down fighting.

The ball squirted out to Bethan who pushed it up into the furthest corner, not tempted to chase it after what happened to Matti. Keep defending was the instruction. Bobby was jumping in frustration, raring to get on and knowing he would have been chasing that ball.

But the No-Hopers still seemed quietly confident. Although the game was not as straightforward as the last time they met this team, there was no real threat of the Ladz scoring a goal. They persevered with their tactics of attack, attack, attack, which the Ladz defended stoically. But Carl and Andy were a spent force, and it was time to roll the dice.

Paul indicated a change while Tiler had the ball. The referee stopped his watch. Timeouts weren't normal but were permissible when the referee thought a team might be wasting time or it was critical to the match. Paul called Carl and Andy off and brought on Gav and, at last, released the angry, hungry, caged tiger. This was the plan – their only plan – their only hope of achieving a win. They'd absorbed everything and were still only two goals down, but time was ticking away, and legs were getting tired.

Paul called Gav to cover the back, Bethan and Ahmed in the middle and Bobby up front. The ref blew to restart the game.

Tiler rolled the ball past the Really Obnoxious One, and it arrived at Ahmed's feet. He knew where Bobby would be, so he hit an incisive pass upfield. Bobby exploded off the halfway line and was on it like an Exocet. He took the No-Hopers completely by surprise as he raced forward, touching the ball with his left foot into his firing zone. There were no deft touches, no niceties or tricks – it was route one – a perfectly hit shot straight into the bottom-right corner that no goalkeeper could have saved. The crowd's banners flew, flags waved madly, and the noise intensified. It was game on. 2–1.

So wound up was Bobby that none of the team dared go near him. 'Well done' and 'Good job, Bobby' was all they gave him from a distance. The No-Hopers were shouting at each other with 'Who should have been there?' and 'Who didn't get back?' types of questions. Paul liked what he was seeing, but he wondered if he'd left it too late.

The No-Hopers kicked off, not daring to try their move again. The Weird One received the kick-off from the Captain, but he was sloppy and under-hit a pass back to the Idiot. He hadn't seen Bobby directly behind him, and Bobby pounced on it, getting to the ball before the Idiot. As the Idiot was moving forward, Bobby easily passed across him going diagonally left. Once past, he turned diagonally right, feinted a shot which the keeper went with, and it was an easy touch in for the Ladz' second goal. The crowd went crazy. There was no one left at the tables. Even Stella had come over to watch – to see her hero scoring. 2–2.

Paul was pleased to see there was more concentration than celebration as the Ladz set back up. They knew they still had a job to do, and that they were getting more tired by the second. That was in stark contrast with their opponents, who were openly at each other's throats.

Paul brought Matti back on for Ahmed, who had run his legs into the ground. 'Come on, Matti,' he shouted. 'You stay middle and try not to let them pass you. You're doing great!' Then, turning to the team with clenched fists, he added for the rest, 'We've done it! We've got them rattled, and the cracks are beginning to show.'

Once again, the No-Hopers kicked off amongst their own recriminations and jibes and resumed their war of attrition. Paul knew they'd be happy with a draw going into extra time, because you didn't need to be Pep Guardiola to see that most of the Ladz were running on fumes. After several minutes in the Ladz' half, a fed-up Bobby Brown came back to claim the ball. Bobby targeted the Really Obnoxious One as he was receiving a pass unbalanced. He pulled the ball back towards himself with his instep and then pushed it through the Really Obnoxious One's legs. 'What the f—?' He didn't have time to finish, as Bobby had exploded into action again. The No-Hopers didn't realise how fast Bobby was over thirty yards. They were all forward, so it was just Bobby against the keeper.

Paul hardly dared to breathe. Could it be possible? Surely not …

But Bobby seemed to have other ideas. Him in competition with a goalkeeper, even one as good as this one, was no competition at all. The sound of the ball hitting the backboards heralded the Ladz' third goal. The crowd was in raptures. They may have a new name on the trophy after all.

It was 3–2 to the Ladz!

'Bobby, Bobby, Bobby!' the spectators were shouting.

With minutes to go, Paul called everyone back to protect their lead.

'Come on, last few minutes. They've lost their heads. We have to do it now – no extra time, or we're sunk. Give it everything!'

The referee had to call timeout, as the No-Hopers were on the brink of a stand-up fight. Only when they had calmed down could he restart the match and his watch. The No-Hopers kicked off for the fourth time that half.

'Concentrate!' shouted the Captain as he took the kick-off.

Paul blinked the sweat from his eyes, every sinew focused on the ball. The No-Hopers pressed forward, trying to get the goal that would take them to extra time, but every through ball was blocked by the tiring Ladz as they managed to get something in the way.

With less than a minute to go, Tiler was at the edge of his area, blocking a cross-field pass with his foot, when he did the unthinkable – his toes crossed the line. At first, Paul thought the referee hadn't seen it, but, with the help of the howling screams of four No-Hopers, a loud blast on the whistle indicated he had. The ref instantly pointed to the penalty spot to the delight of the high-fiving No-Hopers. There was a groan from the crowd; they knew how close the Ladz had come to winning. In extra time, the youth and fitness of the No-Hopers would shine through, and this was their key to getting there.

Paul ran over to Tiler who was banging his fist on the goalpost in despair. The others were holding their head in their hands or bent over, breathing hard. Tiler groaned.

'Damn it! Can't believe I did that, Paul.' He looked at the clock. 'There'll be no time for us to score again after this. Damn it!'

Paul nodded in agreement. He was exhausted and so disappointed. Unusually, he didn't know what to say.

As the referee picked up the ball, Gav jogged over to Tiler and gently shook his shoulders. 'Come on, Tiler. You can do this!'

'What?' Tiler replied.

'Stay with it – it's not over yet,' Gav continued.

A light seemed to appear in Tiler's eyes as he focused in on Gav. 'Yeah, yeah Gav, I'm gonna do it,' Tiler said. Then, with more determination, 'I'm *really* gonna do it!'

Some of the crowd were shouting hopefully for a VAR check; the rest were just shouting for the Ladz. Trev was screaming through the din, 'Choose a side and *go* for it, Tiler!'

Paul heard him. 'Trev says to choose a side and go for it.'

Tiler nodded, took a deep breath and turned to walk back to his goal.

He squared up between the posts as the Captain took the ball from the referee and placed it on the spot. The Captain glanced at the goal, looked Tiler in the eyes and stepped back the three paces allowed. Tiler accepted the challenge with a nod and prepared himself. Feet on the line – arms wide. He leant forward to get as close to the ball as possible. His eyes were pumped wide with adrenaline, and Paul had never seen him so alert, but as Trev had said, Tiler's only chance was to guess correctly. There was absolute silence; everyone knew this kick would decide the match.

The referee blew his whistle. The Captain started forward and, just before impact, Tiler started to move to his left. The Captain cannily side-footed the ball … to Tiler's right.

The grimace on Tiler's face said it all. It was pitiful. Paul had hoped that Tiler had read the Captain – seen through him – but it wasn't to be. These thoughts were flying through Paul's mind when he saw Tiler change the direction of his upper body in mid-air as the ball moved towards its target. It wasn't pretty, but, just short of the line, Tiler reached out as far as possible with his right hand, and the tips of three sausage fingers were enough to divert the ball off its course. It deflected onto the front of the right post and rebounded to a surprised Gav, who could only hack it upfield. Bobby had been in close watching the penalty, so the only one to react was Matti, who was right on the ball and running hard.

The crowd were going crazy as the roller coaster continued. The No-Hopers were pounding the ground behind Matti, breathing down his neck, but Matti was running like a man possessed as the whole team screamed his name. He was two yards from the goal area, but the keeper was cleverly blocking the whole of his goal. Then Matti, as light and sharp as he was, cut an unexpected ninety-degree right, which left the keeper diving and floundering on the floor and Matti on the right wing with an open goal.

Not expecting Matti's sharp turn, the Obnoxious One tripped over the prone keeper, followed by the Weird One. Matti kicked the ball harder than he'd ever kicked a ball before. The goal shook as the ball hit the net and slammed against the backboards. It rebounded out and struck the Really Obnoxious One in the groin as he was following in, doubling him over and leaving him tangled in the messy pile of bodies.

The crowd was loving it. 'Matti, Matti, Matti!' they shouted. Even Matti's mother was joining in.

Liz leaned forward to snap the perfect picture: Matti, jumping high, punching the air in sheer bliss, framed by the Captain and the Idiot shouting and pointing at the ugly heap of bodies Matti had left strewn on the floor behind him.

By the time Matti landed, the full-time whistle had gone. It was all over.

4–2. The Ladz had won.

Paul was elated. Trev's plan had worked. They had given everything, held nothing back and been successful. The crowd, who'd been so invested in the contest, flooded the playing area as the referee left them to it, his job done.

'WELL DONE, FATLADZ!' screamed the tannoy.

There was no space for the Ladz to congratulate each other. The pitch was full of joy and laughter, banners and flags, and shouting and screaming. Paul found Paula and the boys, who were so proud of their dad, and Matti had located his Mum and Michaela. Liz was holding Bethan up, who looked exhausted. Stella had returned to the buffet bar to get ready for the post-match rush, so Bobby was with Tasha and the girls. Tiler found his new lady friend, who threw her arms around his neck.

The other Ladz were all jumping in a circle in raptures of joy. Paul could see they were as spent as he was but still had enough in the tank to celebrate reaching the peak of their huge and challenging mountain. It was the best feeling in the world to beat the team who'd defeated them so heavily before. All his organisation, their efforts and Trev's planning had borne fruit. They were on top of the world.

Paul looked for the No-Hopers' captain to shake his hand. There was no point in carrying on a grudge. As he approached the opposing team, however, they were shrieking at each other, each one blaming the others. Paul had seen post-mortems after matches but never anything like this; it looked on the verge of turning physical. Paul had been right about them falling apart when rattled, and he could see it was unlikely they'd be back. Hearing their nasty jibes, he stopped. 'D'you know what,' he said to himself, 'you lot deserve each other,' and he turned on his heel to get back to the celebrations.

'CAN ALL PLAYERS PROCEED TO THE TOP END OF THE PITCH. ALL PLAYERS TO THE TOP END OF THE PITCH.'

The spectators cleared the designated area, and the Ladz drifted into the space. The Centre manager walked from his desk to the pitch, carrying a beautiful golden statuette similar to the Jules Rimet trophy, the medals, a collapsible table and his radio mic. The crowd was so elated, even he got a cheer! He quickly set up shop and begged for hush.

'I think you'll all agree,' he said into the mic, which was thankfully quieter than the tannoy, 'we've seen a fantastic game of football tonight.' The crowd cheered, and he waited for the noise to die down. 'This team, The FatLadz!, have come from nothing, but today, I think they would have beaten all-comers.'

More cheers.

'First, I'd like to present the losers' medals to'—he paused for dramatic effect—'*the No-Hopers!*'

Silence. The few No-Hopers' supporters had left after Bobby's third goal. And no No-Hopers materialised.

Someone shouted, 'There they go!'

All heads turned towards the main doors. The No-Hopers were leaving the building, still shouting at each other. The Really Obnoxious One flicked up his middle finger to the crowd and shouted something that no one could hear above the jeers and boos.

The Centre manager shook his head in disgust. 'Terrible. Never mind; let's move on. Now, I give you this year's Cup winners. It's … THE FATLADZ!'

The jeers turned to cheers, and the crowd chanted each player's name as the Centre manager handed out the medals in turn. There were also medals for Kev and Trev, and finally it was Paul's turn. He hastily threw the medal round his neck and reached out to take the Cup.

The manager shouted, 'Here's to a new name on the Cup – THE FATLADZ!'

Paul picked up the trophy and, to the cheers, whistles and applause from the crowd, he held it aloft while the whole team behind him jumped for joy. Another great photo opportunity for Liz.

Once the craziness had died down, everyone migrated to the tables to get some drinks in. The Ladz were gathered around their table, taking the plaudits from passers-by.

'Well done, you guys,' said the Bankers' captain. 'Great to see that lot beaten. You executed that plan perfectly.'

'That was the best game of football I've ever seen,' said Ray, surrounded by his carload of colleagues from the EROC. Many others approached to congratulate them, and the Ladz kept beaming at each other and patting their teammates on the back.

'Well done with that penalty save, Tiler,' said Gav.

'Yeah,' replied Tiler, holding up his three heroic fingers. 'It was only when you said that I could really do it that I thought, yeah, I really could.'

'I was lying,' said Gav. 'I never thought for one moment you'd get anywhere near it!'

Everyone collapsed into laughter and that set the tone for the night. There was lots of match talk to start with, and then it turned into a lovely family night with drinks and food, and the kids playing football on the pitch.

Bobby had stayed with his family, as Stella was rushed off her feet at the buffet. Bethan and Liz loved Paul's boys and made a special fuss of Bobby's girls and his wife, as did Paula. Tiler dodged Paul's wry smile as Claudia was explaining how 'George' had taken eighteen seconds off his two-kilometre time in a week!

The Bankers hung around and turned out to be a nice bunch after giving the Ladz such a kicking during their violent match. The Hammers, the DrunkSkunks and P.S.V. had all watched the match too. They were all thrilled the No-Hopers' spell had been broken. There was a general feeling they'd been banished, never to return.

Paul took his time to speak to every player, including Kev, to congratulate them on their performance and stress what they'd achieved in such a short space of time. He also spoke to Trev – the mastermind behind their success. Trev was thrilled with the way things had gone and was thinking of seeing if any local eleven-a-side teams needed a manager, as he'd really enjoyed being involved in football again.

When Gav saw Paul speaking to Trev, he piped up, 'Three cheers for Trev! Hip, hip …' and they gave him three rousing cheers.

Even when asked directly, Paul didn't go into detail about his release from work. He just said Gerry had taken over from him. It was inevitable the whole story would come out eventually, but … it wasn't his place to out Gerry.

As the evening turned to night, people started to leave, saying, 'See you next season,' with lots of goodbyes and congratulations, until it was only the Ladz and their entourage left.

'Time to make a move,' said Andy. 'Some of us have got work tomorrow, y'know.'

Everyone started gathering their kit and kids.

The Centre manager came over. 'Well done, everyone. To say you exceeded my expectations would be an understatement. You gave us a great game of football, followed by a brilliant night. Everyone was so much more upbeat without the shadow of the No-Hopers hanging over the evening. Plus, we made loads of money at the bar!'

Heads turned to the bar, and Paul expected to see Stella there, but she was gone. Good. There would be no hassle tonight. And Bethan could relax. And when Bethan wasn't stressed, everyone else could relax. Paul and the others wandered towards the doors, laughing and joking, mainly at Kev's expense, suggesting different names he could have called his dog. Most of them would have got him beaten up worse!

As one, they stopped. The laughter and the chat stopped. Time stood still. At the lefthand set of doors stood Stella, Bobby's current belle. At the righthand set of doors was Tasha, Bobby's long-suffering wife, with his girls.

In the silence, nobody moved, apart from Carl, who pushed Bobby to the front of the group. He looked back at Bethan, who was staring him down, daring him. He glanced at the team, all fed up with his annoying antics. He looked at Stella. She was looking him in the eye – enticing him, exciting him.

He took a faltering step forward, then another, then some quicker ones. Stella stepped towards him, but her face instantly dropped as Bobby passed her by. Paul could see the hatred in her eyes as she watched Bobby walking to his family. Bethan's words came back to him. 'Men like him never change; they promise everything and give nothing. They use and discard, then they take their lies and move on to the next one.' He watched as Stella turned towards the team, the mascara beginning to run down her cheeks. He thought he saw a moment of vulnerability, then she turned on her heel and disappeared into the night – another wretched victim of the serial philanderer Bobby Brown.

When Bobby put his arms around Tasha and the girls, all the Ladz cheered, except Bethan, whose lower lip was trembling. Liz held her tightly as Bethan's tears flowed.

'Come on, Beth. It's a happy ending,' said Paul.

'I know,' she managed through sobs. 'Happy tears … happy tears.'

When she'd calmed down, Liz announced, 'I'm going to get a pic of you all coming out with the Cup.' She gave Beth's arm a squeeze and ran out.

'Come on, guys,' shouted Carl as they approached the automatic doors. 'Biggest smiles, highest jumps; say CHEEEEEEEEESE!'

They all ran outside and, after a few paces, every one of them was up in the air behind Paul as he held the trophy high above his head. There was the loudest cheer from the whole team and pure happiness on the faces of their families and friends behind them as fists punched the night sky with unbridled joy.

When Liz's flash shattered the darkness for one more brilliant photograph, their ecstatic moment of triumph was perfectly frozen in time forever.

**

Epilogue

It had been a long day. Paul had been in work for twelve hours and was on his way home. Just a few things to get at the supermarket. Walking from the car park, he still had a spring in his step, so the last person he wanted to bump into was Gerry. Paul was surprised to see Gerry sporting a loose-fitting, grey hoodie with matching bottoms and powder blue trainers.

'Paul.'

'Gerry. What's happening?'

'Nothing much,' Gerry replied sullenly.

'You've been off work since the football final, which was over three weeks ago. Nobody's seen you.'

Gerry scratched his chin. 'I can't face coming back, to be honest, Paul. I expect everyone's talking about me. I can't face it.'

Paul couldn't deny that Gerry was a major source for the gossipmongers because he was. Most conversations seemed to end up on the subject of Gerry.

'So, what's happened since?' asked Paul, not really interested.

'Well, that night, after you'd gone, I decided I was going to go home after the shift, get the kids to school and tell my wife. I couldn't live a double life anymore; it was tearing me apart. I knew it wouldn't go well because she's an old-fashioned Irish Catholic. But I never thought it would be quite so brutal. She threw me out immediately and banned me from having anything to do with the children. Called me a disgusting pervert.'

Paul raised his eyebrows. 'Harsh. What did you do?'

'I went to stay with Lawrence for a few nights. He wanted me to move in – still does – but it's too soon. I've got to sort things out at home before I try and move on. Probably end up going down the legal route, I expect.'

'Oh,' said Paul, completely nonplussed by this unexpected conversation.

'The council found me a bedsit over the shops, and that's where I'm up to.'

'Have you been in touch with the company?'

Gerry nodded. 'They've been very good, very understanding. They've told me to take as long as I want and have put me in touch with some specialist counsellors. They've supported hundreds of people struggling with this very situation. They're going to help me, quote, "find myself", unquote.'

It was strange for Paul having a conversation with Gerry where no one was shouting or angry. He thought maybe all this would benefit Gerry in the long run if he could accept himself and sort out his homelife.

'How are things in work?'

'Good. I've been covering your job while you've been away, so there's no need to rush back.'

'You're better cut out for that job than me, Paul. I should never have taken it. I can't come back.' Gerry paused. 'Everyone all right after the football?'

'Yeah. Emily, Daniel's daughter, came out of hospital after four days. It was touch and go, apparently.'

'Shit. What a twat I was,' Gerry said, colour rising to his cheeks. 'Daniel's a good one, and I was like the school bully. That's why I can't come back – too many bridges to build.'

'Mmm,' agreed Paul, 'but the good news is he starts filming in November for *MasterChef*.'

'Brilliant! He's a great cook. I'm sure he'll do well.'

'Lawrence gave up the whole of the National Newsletter to us with pictures, and our story was in the *Echo* too, so that was nice.'

Gerry smiled. 'He said he'd worked hard on it.'

'What else? Carl was over the moon to finally get the gym bench-press record, with no questions asked this time.'

'Wow'—Paul had never heard Gerry say 'wow' before—'that's really something. Not surprised, though; those shoulders are like Arnie's!'

'True. Trev's been taken on by the YMCA as assistant coach to their football teams. He's so much livelier now, loving being back in football.'

'… where he always belonged.'

Paul nodded. 'Exactly where he belongs. I can see him going further than that, the way he managed our team, the training, the drills, the gameplans, the knowledge and the presence; he's got it all. He's talking about doing his FA coaching badges too.'

'Awesome!'

'What else?' Paul said, a hand to his forehead. 'Andy's still sneaking up on people. Getting his old Army kit out has inspired him to get back in touch with some of his military buddies. They're organising a get-together next month. Kev's still doing stupid things. Oh, and Sam's put in for a transfer to be based with us in the CROC all the time. Ahmed's on track to set up his garage business, just waiting for his grant to come through.'

'I was horrible to him – it was the stress – it was too much – I couldn't deal with it, Paul. I realised that night that all you were saying was true, and that was what broke down my wall.'

Paul nodded and carried on. 'Tiler's as happy as Larry, oops … sorry!' They both laughed. Paul had never seen Gerry laugh unless it was at someone else's expense. 'He's got himself a lady friend from the running club, which is ironic because he was totally anti-running when we started discussing what we should do to get fit!'

'Tiler happy and with a girlfriend. Things have really come round in the CROC.'

'Yeah. Beth and her partner, Liz, were so taken with Bobby's children, they're going to get married this year and have a baby. Beth is absolutely beside herself with happiness.'

'Nice. And what of the Casanova Bobby Brown?'

'He hasn't returned to work after the football, either. Taken all his holidays. My wife saw him in town last week with his family; they seemed happy when she spoke to them. Hopefully, he'll be "finding himself" too.'

'Maybe he's matured.'

'Maybe,' said Paul doubtfully. 'Then there's Matti – Sebastian. He seems well enough now after the company set him up with some counselling, but you can never tell with that stuff.'

'No, you can't.'

'He's got to decide whether to move on or stay with us for another three months. He wants to stay, but Trev's told him to get out and see the rest of the company to find out what suits him best. Not sure what he'll do.'

'He's a nice kid. He must think I'm a right arsehole.'

Again, Paul didn't contradict Gerry; that was exactly what Matti thought. 'Since he's been with us, he's come on leaps and bounds at home and in work, so his mother doesn't want him to leave either. We've recreated that sense of community, of belonging, that's been missing for so long, and he's a part of that, part of a team with, well, family spirit.'

Gerry sighed. 'No thanks to me.'

'But that's what I wanted more than anything else – to rebuild the community spirit. It seems management have the same vision, as they've made me the health and welfare champion for the ROCs. I've got a budget and lots of ideas, so when you come back, you can get involved.' Gerry seemed in need of a bit of encouragement for the future.

'I won't be coming back, Paul.'

'But—'

'No. When you set up the football, you threw a stone into a

pond, and the ripples have affected so many people for the better. I'm struggling now, but this was eventually going to happen; our quarrel just accelerated things. This is also going to be for the better, but it's difficult while I'm sorting things out. I'm not a people person; you are. I've asked them to find me a job in an office with a computer. Maybe I'll feel different eventually.' He added thoughtfully, 'No, I already feel different – like a weight's been taken off my shoulders. So, as difficult as they were to hear, thanks for your honest words that night. Things will work out for me now. I know it.'

'Well, take it easy, Gerry.'

'Yeah. I'll see you round, I expect.'

With a slight nod of his head, Gerry turned and walked away.

Paul watched him go. 'Gerry,' he called.

Gerry turned. There was a pause.

'Keep in touch.'

Again, the slight nod of the head, and Gerry was on his way, looking taller and lighter on his feet. Paul thought about the ripples in the pond. Gerry was right, the ROC world was a much better place for what Paul had achieved.

As Gerry disappeared around the corner, Paul turned towards the shopping centre. He walked on, the spring in his step a little higher.

***

·

Author's Note

Although inspired by a real event, this book is clearly a work of fiction based around the environment of a modern-day signalling centre and its imaginary group of workers. It is not meant to detract in any way from the amazing work performed by many people in many different roles who try so hard to keep our railways running. Often working in difficult conditions, they arrive with one aim: keep both passengers and freight as safe and punctual as possible.

Day after day they deal diligently with many differing situations, all of which have the potential to delay, damage or derail. It is a credit to all railway personnel that accidents and incidents are few and far-between on our busy infrastructure.

This is not a textbook and the over-lying story comes from my imagination. It does not imply that this is the way such signalling centres are run in the real world.

Neil Quinn
2025

Printed in Dunstable, United Kingdom

72080366R10116